THE DARK

OTHER BOOKS BY ANTHONY GIANGREGORIO

THE DEAD WATER SERIES

DEADWATER
DEADWATER: Expanded Edition
DEADRAIN
DEADCITY
DEADWAVE
DEAD HARVEST
DEAD UNION

ALSO BY THE AUTHOR

DEAD RECKONING: DAWNING OF THE DEAD
THE MONSTER UNDER THE BED
DEADEND: A ZOMBIE NOVEL
DEAD TALES: SHORT STORIES TO DIE FOR
DEAD MOURNING: A ZOMBIE HORROR STORY
ROAD KILL: A ZOMBIE TALE
DEADFREEZE
DEADFALL
DEADRAGE
SOUL-EATER
RISE OF THE DEAD
DARK PLACES

THE DARK

ANTHONY GIANGREGORIO

The Dark

Copyright © 2009 by Anthony Giangregorio

ISBN   Softcover ISBN 13: 978-1-935458-03-6
                         ISBN 10: 1-935458-03-5

This is a work of fiction. Names, characters, places and incidents either are the product of the author's imagination or are used fictitiously, and any resemblance to any actual persons, living or dead, events, or locales is entirely coincidental.

This book was printed in the United States of America.

For more info on obtaining additional copies of this book, contact:
www.livingdeadpress.com

ACKNOWLEDGEMENTS

As always, my wife Jody and my son, Joseph deserve a big thanks. Whether it's listening to my next 'great' idea or reading the same story for the third time, they are always there for me. They are my writer's support group, and half of what I have accomplished is thanks to them.

AUTHOR'S NOTE

This book was self-edited, and though I tried my absolute best to correct all grammar mistakes, there may be a few here and there. Please accept my sincerest apology for any errors you may find.

Visit my website at undeadpress.com

1

THE SIREN

I WAS FAST when the siren first began to wail, slicing the air with its shrill scream, foretelling everyone of the doom to come.

At first I stayed in bed, not wanting to get up and see what was happening. I wasn't worried, figuring the stupid thing was probably broken.

It had happened before.

It was about three years ago, give or take, when it happened the last time. Forgive me if I don't know the exact date and time. The siren had gone off for almost an hour before someone had the bright idea to simply cut the power. Boy, there were a lot of disgruntled senior citizens calling into city hall that day.

The siren was what in the Middle Ages would have been a church bell, rung to let the surrounding populace know there was something wrong; the town crier without the crying. But now, in the twentieth century, the siren merely went off at noon and eight p.m., just in case someone didn't own a clock and needed to know what time it was.

So here I was on the first day of my vacation and I wasn't allowed to sleep because of a malfunctioning siren.

I could hear my wife downstairs in the kitchen, and my son, Kyle, was there as well. Actually, I could have heard my son if he was on the moon and was talking softly under a pillow. My son has more energy than every nuclear reactor combined. I mean, this kid will go to bed at midnight and be up, wide eyed and bushy tailed at six the next morning, watching cartoons and munching on an apple. Not me though. I need a good ten hours of sleep before I can even think about functioning in the real world.

And this morning, with the siren screaming its noise that something was up, I was only clocking in about eight hours or so.

My wife's voice could be heard in tandem to my son's, and it was then that I realized she was on the telephone.

Good, I thought, maybe she's complaining about that damn siren. Might as well be one of the first to get our licks in because once the seniors get going, the phone lines will be jammed for the rest of the day.

We lived in the city, actually, but there were more geriatrics than in most towns that I knew of.

The city of Revere, in good old Massachusetts, was about six miles from Boston. It wasn't a bad place to live in, actually. It was the kind of place where the Walmart was down the street, but yet you still had grass on the sidewalks, Sure, parts of the city looked like an ad for urban renewal, but there were other parts that had old oak trees lining the sidewalks, their thick trunks almost as wide as the walks themselves. Not to mention their roots, which grew so big the cement of the sidewalk resembled a roller coaster and you had to be careful if you went for a stroll after dinner.

And the seniors. Well, more than half the city was still filled with the settlers of fifty plus years ago. When the old folks got too old to take care of themselves or their homes, they merely moved into one of the dozen or so nursing homes or assisted living complexes. Hell, over by the beach, historic Revere Beach, that is, with its soda cans and seaweed and plastic bags buried in the sand, there were three high-rises built just to hold the senior citizens.

By now you're probably wondering how old I am if I talk about seniors as old. I'm in my late thirties and figure seventy is still a long way off. My wife is actually three years older than me and I always like to tease her about it. Karen will sometimes feel a little down that she's hit the big 4-0 and I tell her. "Hey, look at the bright side?" And she would always ask me what that might be and I'd tell her. "At least I'm only thirty seven." She would usually throw a pillow at me then or just flash me one of her patented frowns and say to me. "You're not that far off, John Russell, you'll be there soon enough." I would usually begin to chuckle and would wander away, smug in the fact I was still in my thirties.

So to me, seventy is still a long way off.

The siren was still shrieking bloody murder and my wife's voice was rebounding off the kitchen walls downstairs like she was trying to sing along with the siren. The front door was being opened and then slammed repeatedly and I finally decided I should get up and see what the hell was going on.

It was morning after all and bright sunlight was flooding through the open window shades like there was a spotlight aimed at my house, courtesy of God Himself.

After sliding into my robe, I hit the bathroom quickly and headed downstairs. At least there was the smell of coffee, telling me things weren't all bad.

The instant my foot struck the first floor landing, Karen was in my face, her visage filled with what seemed to be concern and somewhere below that perhaps just a little bit of fear.

"Oh, John, I was just about to wake you, thank God you got up," she said in a frazzled voice. Kyle was standing beside her, one eye on me and the other on the front door, like he was a sentinel to the Holy Grail.

I rubbed my face with my hands and yawned heavily as I stared at her worried countenance. "What Karen, what's wrong," I asked her flatly, for me there was nothing wrong except my lack of sleep.

"There's something happening in New York. I was on the phone talking with my mother and the phone cut out." Karen's mother lived in upstate New York and we would visit her two or three times a year, taking the Mass Turnpike.

"So, use your cell phone," I told her. "Call her back on that." Sometimes my wife needed to be told the simplest things. It wasn't that she was stupid; it was just sometimes she couldn't see the forest for the trees.

She flashed me a depreciating frown as if I had just insulted her.

"Don't you think I know that? I tried and there's no service for some reason."

"What about the TV? Surely the news knows something."

She shook her head, her brown tresses cascading around her shoulders. "No, they're talking about it, but they don't really know anything, either."

I nodded at that statement. Whenever any crisis happened, the news would rush to get there and then report about it, despite the fact they would have no clue what was really going on. In times like that you could get a different telling of events from each channel until the crisis was finally over and the authorities began piecing together what had happened. But still, each news company could brag that they, "Were the first to get there and tell us nothing," or something to that effect.

"Daddy, what's going on? Why is that horn making all that noise?" Kyle asked from beside his mother's legs.

I looked down at him, a smile across my lips. Whatever was happening outside, I needed to act calm. Hell, it was my job as a parent. It could be World War 3 outside my door and I would look my son straight in the eye and tell him everything was fine. It was just one of the dozens of white lies a parent tells their child to keep them feeling safe and secure.

"Everything is fine, Kyle, I promise. Say, tell you what, why don't you set up the checker board and I'll let you try and beat me after I'm done talking to your mother."

Kyle made a raspberry as if that would be the last thing that would happen, but his eyes lit up with anticipation and he trotted off to the den to gather the checkers and board. Actually, his doubt wasn't far from the truth. My son appeared to be a prodigy when it came to checkers. Now, I don't mean he was the best player in the world, I just think it's great that at his age he already knows all the rules. And many times he actually beats me if I'm not really concentrating. He especially likes it when I'm talking on the phone as I can't focus on the game.

One of these days, I'll have to introduce him to chess. If he took to chess like he does to checkers, he just might end up being some kind of boy wonder or a genius someday. A prodigy grown from my loins, now that would be something to brag about to your friends and neighbors. It sure beats one of those stupid bumper stickers that declares that I have a son on the honor roll at something-something middle school.

I heard voices coming from out in the street and I went to the front door, unlocking and opening it. There were more than a dozen people outside, most gathered in groups of threes and fours. I saw my next door neighbor, Fred Harper, and his wife, Margie. They were surrounded by three other people and it seemed Fred had them all wrapped up in whatever he was telling them. Some of the people were still in their pajamas and robes like I was, so I didn't give it much thought as I walked outside wearing my bathrobe and slippers.

It was a bright mid-summer's morning, and it looked like when it hit noon in a few hours it would be a good day for the beach. In the background, coming from about a mile away, the siren continued to screech its warning.

Was it me or did everyone's faces seem worried? Not that I blamed them. That damn siren was like a dog whistle to the canines of the world. Hearing that screeching tone just made you feel like something was going to happen. It gave me a small idea what it must have been like in London during World War 2 when the bombs would be dropping, the air raid horn the only warning the population would get before their homes were blasted to ash and fire.

I walked over to Fred's group and Margie nodded as I approached. Behind me, Karen stayed at our door, not wanting to leave Kyle alone in the house.

"Hello, John, have you heard what's happening?" Margie asked, her voice fluttering with excitement.

I told her no and she was kind enough to elaborate.

"Well, Fred was lucky enough to get through to the police before the phone lines went down. It appears New York is gone."

"What?" I sneered. "What do you mean, gone? You mean like an explosion? Oh God, it's not another terrorist attack is it?" Vivid images of 9-11 came flooding back and I felt my insides go numb and the hair stand up on the back of my neck like porcupine quills.

Margie shook her head. "No, John, no one thinks so, but..."

That was all she got out because Fred had spun around, seeing me for the first time, and having caught a small tidbit of what Margie was telling me, he dove in with his own story, cutting his wife off in mid-sentence. He was in luck; he had told everyone on the street the same story and now had a fresh audience with me. Fred was one of those men who would talk to a mirror if no one else was around to speak to. Fred was in his late sixties, maybe a year shy of seventy. He had silver hair and a friendly face. He was the kind of person almost anyone would feel comfortable chatting with. He would take walks around supper time and chat with everyone he met. He said you find out what's happening in your neighborhood when you walk it. Driving, you see nothing.

"No, John, it's not terrorists, or at least the police didn't think so. I was in luck when I called the station. You know Ben who lives on K Street? Well, it was his son who answered the phone. He's been on the force for almost a year now. I used to take him apple picking every summer with my son when he was young, so when he knew it was me on the other end of the line he…"

"Focus, Fred, focus, what about New York?" I asked him impatiently. Now was not the time for him to wander off topic. Fred had a way about him. Instead of answering a question with a simple yes or no, he would tell you a story for the next five minutes about how he had weighed the question and finally decided to go with yes for an answer. By the time he was finished telling you his answer, you would usually end up forgetting what you had asked him in the first place or you just wouldn't care anymore.

"Huh, what? Oh sorry, John. Well, as I was saying, Ben's son, Steve, said that there seems to be some kind of black wall completely surrounding New York City and get this, it's spreading."

"What do you mean, it's spreading?" This came from another neighbor of mine. His name was Ted Gardner and he lived four houses down from me. I didn't talk to Ted much. He had a shabby looking house and never cut his grass. Call me a small person, but I get really pissed off when one of my neighbors doesn't take care of his house. It wasn't like Ted was an isolated incident. In Revere, there were at least one or two houses on every street that looked like they were abandoned. High grass, peeling paint and usually the two or three cars with flat tires and rusted out fenders that hadn't been registered to be on the road legally since 1980. Not to mention the houses that had sheets for curtains, those were always my favorite. So me and Ted weren't exactly best buds. Not able to keep my mouth closed, I had asked him a few times to cut his grass when it had reached knee high and was falling over like a drunk at last call. He had promptly told me to go screw myself and so a feud was born.

Fred turned to Ted, nodding that what he was saying was exactly what was happening and Ted was a fool to doubt him.

"That's what I said, it's spreading. Steve said every hour or so it spreads another inch."

"So what is it?" A woman asked. She lived across the street, five or so homes down. I didn't know her at all, but only knew she lived on my street because I would pass her by in her yard when I went to work. I didn't even know if she was married or what her name was. All I knew was that she was a mail carrier for the city as I'd seen her bring the postal truck home during lunch time. On second thought, I think she was married or something like marriage, but it was to another woman. I think she was a lesbian, but the butch kind, not that it mattered much. I'm all for gay love, but prefer it when the two women are really hot, the two butch ones, not so much.

I wasn't even listening to Fred as he rambled on. I turned at the sound of Karen calling my name and saw she was still at the front door. She had moved a few feet away from it, but it was like she was tethered to it, an invisible chain holding her from straying too far from the doorway. When she saw I had seen her, she waved for me to come back to the house. I listened for another second about what Fred was saying and decided that was about all I was going to get from either Fred or any of the other neighbors. I turned to walk away, and just as I moved the first three steps, Fred stopped talking to the others and called to me.

"Hey, John, a few of the guys and I are gonna go to Stern's Hardware and the supermarket, want to come? Figure we should get some extra stuff while the gettin's good."

I hesitated for a second, giving that some thought and decided I'd pass.

"That's okay, Fred, I'll go myself in a little while. Besides, I've got some other errands to run."

Fred nodded. "Sure enough, but listen, it'll be in another hour or so before we head out. We just want to make sure we know everything that's going on before we leave, so if you change your mind..." He trailed off like he was wont to do.

"Okay, I'll remember that, Fred, thanks."

I waved politely and headed back to my house, the others in the street still talking back and forth. A police car screamed down the street running perpendicular to mine. I was just able to see it for a brief moment when it sped by, then its siren faded away to be lost with the background noise of the fire station siren. That damn siren was really beginning to annoy me; after all, what was the point in keeping it on for such a long time? Pretty much everyone in hearing distance knew something was up, so what would keeping it on accomplish?

Shaking my head about the irrational humans I inhabit the planet with, I crossed my front lawn, climbed the three steps that led to my front porch and stopped when I had reached my waiting wife.

"There's something on the TV, John, I thought you might want to see it."

"Yeah, I do," I said to her as I followed her back into the house. Behind me, Fred droned on about what he thought he knew and most definitely about what he didn't.

2

THE NEWS

KYLE WAS PLAYING in the den and looked up as I walked into the kitchen through the front door. He jumped up from the small storage box we used as a coffee table in the den and ran to me, his eyes glittering with happiness.

"Hi, Daddy, are you ready to play checkers yet? They're all set up. I'm gonna be white."

I patted his head like a dog and smiled down at him.

"Sure, champ, just let me watch something on the news first."

Kyle nodded and took off back into the den, running full tilt despite the fact the distance was less than twelve feet. I watched him go and expected him, like I always did, to crash into the entertainment center holding the television, but he did a controlled re-entry and shifted his shoulder, missing the piece of furniture by inches. Then he leaped into the air and came down hard on the couch, the couch springs groaning from the pressure. Normally, I would have chastised him for doing this, but the news was more important. Actually, with what was happening in New York, a lot of things I thought were important seemed to be very trivial right now.

Karen went to the TV and turned up the volume and we both sat down at the kitchen table, watching the twelve-inch screen. An attractive woman news reporter was standing with her microphone in her hand, and as the wind whipped her dark hair around her head like a cyclone, she continued to talk.

"I'm standing here on the outskirts of New York City in front of what scientists have simply nicknamed The Dark. So far, from what we've been able to ascertain, none have an inkling as to what this could be. There have been assumptions that this strange wall of darkness which has swallowed New York whole is some after affect of the solar eclipse we experienced last week; despite the fact no other such occurrence was scheduled."

I thought back to what the woman was saying. Last week there had been a solar eclipse and I remembered fondly how amazed Kyle had been when the sun had seemed to disappear like magic and how the street had been thrown into darkness. We even made a viewing box out of an old shoe box.

The newswoman turned around, letting the camera scan across the edge of what could only be called a massive wall of darkness. The camera went high, all the way straight up, and still the wall continued. If I had to guess at it, I'd say it must have gone straight into the atmosphere. It was amazing, even despite the terror of the unknown. The wall of darkness was perfectly vertical, like a cheese cube having been cut by a wire. To say it defied the laws of physics would be an understatement. Whenever a spotlight or light of any kind was pointed at the wall, the light would simply stop, as if it had been absorbed by a sponge. Men in white jumpsuits were running along the wall, holding all kinds of technical gear. I spotted one such item and was fairly certain it was a Geiger counter. That sent a shiver down my spine as I thought about the relevance if the darkness was somehow radioactive. When we were kids most of us feared the dark, afraid there was something ominous moving about in the obsidian void, but this was something on a whole new level.

Besides the men in white suits, there were dozens of police cars and large vans which I only assumed contained technical gear. Military humvees and cargo vans painted in camouflage colors were everywhere. It was utter, yet controlled, chaos as men and women ran about as if they had a purpose. I couldn't help but wonder if any of them truly knew what they were doing or what they were dealing with.

I listened as the reporter continued talking.

"No one has been able to talk to or receive any signals from New York or its outlying provinces since this abnormality appeared a few hours ago." She stopped talking, listening to her earpiece for a second and then after a quick nod, resumed speaking. "I've just gotten word that one of our news copters is about to enter the wall of darkness. We'll go now to them high above us, Bill?"

The camera flickered and the picture on the screen was of a helicopter pilot. Behind him was nothing but blue, and when the cameraman turned to point the lens out the front windshield of the helicopter, the wall came into view. The entire screen was nothing but blackness while the pilot spoke in the background, the sounds of the rotors making him have to yell.

"This is Bill Donaldson for Eyewitness News and I'm about to enter the wall of darkness. So far, I've been unable to receive any radio signals from inside this strange occurrence, so that is the reason why I've decided to fly in despite stern warnings from both civil and military authorities. I want it known that I have chosen to do this on my own accord and the news station should not be held responsible for my actions."

"Then why are you doing this, Bill? Why don't you let the military handle it?" A voice asked, overriding Bill's. I could tell it was the voice of the female reporter who had first been on the screen. The camera went from the wall of darkness to the pilot's face. Bill looked serious as he stared back at the viewers at home.

"Why? I'll tell you why. This is what I became a reporter for. This is the reason I got my pilot's license, to be part of something grander than myself." He turned away from the camera and stared at the obsidian wall. "This is something big, I can feel it and I want to be the first one to see what's inside. Okay, We're going in, hold on tight, Bruce." I could only assume Bruce was the cameraman. The screen filled with Bill's face as he aimed the helicopter towards the wall. The cameraman--Bruce, I now called him--turned the camera to record the wall again. Karen and I watched in awe as the ebony wall grew larger and larger and then the screen went black. It took me a moment to realize that there was no picture or sound.

"Bill? Bill, are you there?" The reporter asked, only mild concern in her voice. The camera went back to the reporter and a concerned look was on her face. "Uhm, we seemed to have lost Bill Donaldson," she said apologetically with just a hint of a tremor in her voice. But she knew better than to look shaken. She was a professional and would remain one for as long as possible. "Wait a second, something seems to be happening." She turned around and the cameraman followed her gaze. The dark wall seemed to pulse and then it moved, sliding across the land like a giant plow. Chaos ensued as men, women and equipment tried to get out of the way, some trying to move the valuable equipment with little or no luck. The wall moved more than ten feet, growing so fast many were not able to get out of the way in time. What was weird was there were no screams of pain as the wall overran the people not fast enough to escape it. It was quite silent actually. One second they were standing there on the ground, and then, bam, they were gone, the wall of darkness now on top of the land they once occupied.

"Jesus Christ, what the hell just happened?" The news reporter yelled as she stared at the growing wall." She turned to the cameraman. "Come on, Bobby, we need to move away from this before it does that again. I don't know what happened to those people, but I'm not gonna be next." Then she realized she was still live and tried to regain her composure. "Oh, uhm, this is Rosanne Rodriquez signing off for channel six news."

The screen flicked back to the newsroom, the two manicured anchormen sitting behind their desks. I watched for a few more minutes and then, realizing the anchors were just talking shit, not having anymore of a clue of what had just happened than any of us watching did, I decided to turn it off.

"Oh my God, John, what are we gonna do?" Karen asked; the fear in her eyes apparent. "My mother's in there somewhere."

I didn't have an answer for her. Truth was; I was still trying to digest what I'd just witnessed. It was amazing and terrifying all at the same time. There were the beginnings of butterflies in my stomach now. It was the feeling you get when something bad is going to happen. I believe the correct term is; waiting for the other shoe to drop.

"Now, Karen," I said, "don't go getting crazy on me. I'm sure your mother's fine. Besides, this is happening in New York, not here. I mean, it's terrible and all, but what exactly can we do about it?"

"Well still, we need to stock up on the essentials just in case this thing spreads. Oh my God, what if that happens, John? What if that thing comes here? To Boston?"

"Shhh," I whispered in a soft but stern voice. "We'll be fine. Now don't go getting all hysterical on me. Think of Kyle at least. He needs to think everything's okay. You know he'll get scared if you start running around like a chicken with its head cut off."

As if on cue, Kyle stuck his head into the kitchen. "Hey, Daddy, are we gonna play checkers or what?"

I turned around and flashed my son my best smile. "Sure, son, I'm coming right now. Warm up those checkers for me."

He nodded and his head disappeared like a Jack-in-the-box in reverse. I turned to Karen and placed a hand on each of her shoulders, trying to look confidant and sure of myself.

"Look, honey, we're fine here, everything is fine. Whatever's happening is a long way from here. All we can do is pray your mother got out in time and maybe she'll call you in a while from Springfield. In a little while I'll go to the store and get you a few things. Tell you what; I'll grab some extra batteries and candles at the hardware store, too, just in case, all right?"

She nodded, her face calming slightly. I leaned forward and kissed her softly. Just a small peck on the lips. But it worked its magic and she seemed to melt in my arms.

"Good, that's good, honey. Now I'm starving, could I impose on you to make me a couple of eggs?"

She nodded. "Sure, John, I can do that."

"Thanks. I'll be in the den whipping our son's butt in checkers." I said this louder than I needed to so Kyle would hear me.

"Fat chance you will, Daddy," Kyle called back.

Chuckling, I turned away from Karen and headed for the den. As I walked away from her, Karen put the news back on. I wasn't happy about that. Sometimes all the news did was make you more afraid than you needed to be. That was their job. The more afraid you were, the more you watched, all the time hoping there might be some small shred of information that might save the day. Unfortunately, just like on 9-11, that rarely happened.

3

CHECKERS WITH KYLE

CAR TROUBLE

"NO FAIR, DADDY, how did you do that?" Kyle asked me as I pushed my checker to the end of the board. He stared at it like it was going to sprout a mouth and bite him. He picked up one of my captured checkers next to him on the floor and placed it on my new king. The double checker was only one of two others on the board, all mine, and the three taller kings seem to hover over the other, regular checkers, like gods from Olympus.

This was our third game and I was beginning to grow bored. Now, maybe it's wrong to say that as a parent, and if it is, I'm sorry, but playing checkers with a seven-year-old can get tiring real fast. Yes, I love spending time with my son, but as a regular human male, I like a challenge, and playing checkers with Kyle is most definitely not a challenge. I think it's because he's not really worried about winning.

I think he just likes playing the game with his old man.

"Look, champ, why don't we call it quits for the time being, your old dad has to run a few errands for your mom."

His eyes lit up with expectation. "Really? I want to come. Can I come, too?" I swear to God if my son had a tail right then he would have begun to wag it.

I gave his question a moment's thought and decided, sure, why not. It'll give us more of that father, son, bonding stuff Dr. Spock--or some other know-it-all who probably doesn't even have kids but yet still knows what's best for me and mine--thinks so highly of.

Climbing to my feet, I headed into the kitchen, Kyle right behind me like a puppy.

"Get your sneakers on, sport; I just want to talk to your mom for a sec'." He nodded and took off for the small mudroom at the back of the house, where we keep all the shoes and sneakers.

Karen was still at the kitchen table, her legs level and tight, her inner thighs touching one another. Her face looked pale and her eyes were riveted to the television screen, almost as if she was hypnotized. I knew better than to ask her if anything new had happened. If it had, she would have immediately called out to me to come and see.

"Hey, Karen," I said to her, but she acted like she didn't hear me. Deciding I needed a better approach, I moved in front of the TV so she had no choice but to look at me. "Karen, are you all right?"

"I'm fine, John, now please move out of the way, you're blocking the television."

"No kidding, I'm blocking it." I sighed heavily. "Look, why don't you go take a shower or something? Take a break for a little while. I have a feeling you won't miss anything," I suggested this with a calm voice though something inside me wanted to yell at her, shake her like a rag doll to cut the shit and turn the damn set off. My wife did the same thing on 9-11. The news was on twenty-four/seven, with never a break. I had to make her turn it off when we had sex or I swear she would have been watching the news over my shoulder while we made love.

She looked up at me and I could see her eyes were red from crying. "John, what if what's happening in New York comes here? What will we do? My God, John, where have all those people gone that are inside the darkness? Why can't we get a hold of them? My Mom?"

I walked across the room and placed my hands on her shoulder, pulling her close to me. She leaned her head against my stomach and we stayed that way for a few moments, lost in the comfort of one another. Her mother meant a lot to her, more so than others might know. Her father had died more than twenty years ago of cancer and the two of them had only had each other to lean on.

"What about Kyle, John? What will happen to Kyle if that thing comes here?"

"That won't happen, Karen, I know it won't." But deep down in my gut, I could only pray my words were truthful and not the wishful thinking of a desperate man.

"Look, just promise me you'll stop watching the news every damn minute, please? As for Kyle, well, he's coming with me to the supermarket. That should keep him busy for a little while and give you a few minutes alone. Now, why don't you make me a list of what you want me to get."

She nodded, her face brushing my belt buckle. In between the second and third game with Kyle I had gotten dressed.

Then Kyle charged back inside and I turned away from Karen, with one last hug to comfort her.

"Ready, Daddy," Kyle called, his face excited to go out with his old man. Once again, I thought how he looked like a puppy, sans wagging tail. His eyes were wide and his light brown hair was hanging over his forehead, his high cheek bones showing off his ancestry. When he smiled, he had a missing tooth, a casualty of the tooth fairy, actually. Three days ago he had bitten into an apple and the tooth had popped out with a little blood. To him it had been a tragedy of epic proportions. That was his blood on the apple and that was terribly wrong. His blood was supposed to stay inside him where it belonged. But after some ice cream and a promise of a visit from the tooth fairy with cold, hard cash, he had calmed down, and five minutes after the incident occurred he was sitting in the den again watching SpongeBob like the event had never happened. Ah, the resilience of youth.

To an adult, something like that would have required weeks of therapy and self discovery, well all right, maybe I'm over doing it a little, but I think you get my point.

So as I stared at my son, a part of my own flesh and blood, from across the kitchen and I felt such love and pride for the person he was already becoming. Kyle was a caring, loving, little boy who was respectful of others. I swear he didn't have a mean bone in his body.

"Daddy, did you hear me? I'm ready to go." He looked to Karen and his smile faltered. "Is Mommy okay? Why's she crying?"

I snapped out of the little reverie I had fallen into and smiled at him. "Sure, champ, I'm ready to leave. Mommy's fine, she just saw something sad on the TV. Come here and give your mom a kiss before we go."

He did so, once again running the few feet to Karen instead of walking, the energy inside him needing to be expelled or he would end up exploding like a nuclear reactor in meltdown. She hugged and kissed him and then he broke free. Without a backwards glance, he charged for the back door and the driveway waiting beyond. I followed, and when I reached the backdoor, I turned to wave goodbye to Karen, but she was already lost in the news again, some nameless face trying to make sense of something that may quite possibly never make sense.

Kyle was doing laps in the driveway, running around the car like he was an all-star on the school track team. He usually did something like this. Sometimes he would grab his scooter and zip back and forth as many times as he could squeeze in before I told him we had to go. Kyle was a sheltered boy by today's standards. While his schoolmates were running around in the streets and going to the park alone; some of them already walking back and forth to school unattended, Kyle was watched like a hawk. There were far too many predators out there on the streets for me to just let him wander around on his own. Whether these other parents didn't love their children as much as I did mine or the fact they were simply ignorant of the dangers a young child faces, the facts were there. I know the odds of Kyle ever being taken off the street while he was playing was slim, but I bet if you ever asked one of the parents of a missing child how they felt about those odds, I'd bet they'd tell you to go to hell. When your child is the one out of a million that is taken or killed, the odds really don't matter that much anymore. And so that was why my wife picked him up and dropped him off at school everyday.

I watched Kyle for another second and then went to open the door of my car. It was an old Ford Taurus. I had moved ninety percent of my house years ago inside this car instead of renting a moving truck and was quite fond of it. When it comes to cars, I mate for life, or the life of the car before it finally goes belly up.

"Come on, Kyle, its time to go!" I called out as I rolled down the driver's side window. It was a crank window, not electric, just one of the many necessities I live without. The radio is a tape deck instead of a CD player and there's no air conditioning, which can be a problem in the warm New England summers. But I survive. I usually plug a small fan into the cigarette lighter to keep me cool on my way to and from work.

"Okay, Daddy, I'm, coming," Kyle said as he zipped by the car and let the scooter keep going until it fell over onto the grass. Then he ran to the side door and climbed inside.

I turned the ignition to start the motor and was surprised when nothing happened.

"What the?" I said, with curiosity. I tried again, but all I got was one dull click. Reaching over to the dash, I tried the radio and frowned even more when it failed to come on.

"Shit, the damn battery is dead," I muttered.

"Uh-oh, Daddy, you said a swear word," Kyle said from the back seat.

"Please, Kyle, not now, there's something wrong with the car." I said this with a little too much anger in my voice, none of it aimed at Kyle, but he still took the brunt of it.

"Sorry, Daddy, I'll be quiet," he said meekly.

Now I felt like a jerk, picking on my seven-year-old son. "No, champ, I'm sorry, I'm not mad at you. Just let me check a few more things out, okay?"

He nodded and picked up an action figure of some wrestler he liked. I didn't let him watch wrestling, but he still heard about it in school from his friends. The toy came from one of them, a prize he'd brought home from school one day. I was meaning to make the toy disappear when he went to bed, but hadn't gotten around to it.

I checked a few more items over, the signal lights, the headlights, the dashboard lights. Hell, even the cigarette lighter, and it was pretty obvious to anyone who knew how to drive a car the battery was dead.

"Dammit," I said, punching the steering wheel. Then I re-membered Kyle in the back seat and controlled my temper. With a weary sigh leaving my lips, I opened the driver's door.

"Come on, sport, we're not going anywhere in this car today."

"What's wrong, Daddy? Are you out of gas? You should check the gas level."

He asked me this in such a cute but serious voice, like he was a mechanic diagnosing the problem. His face was just so serious when he suggested it had to be that, it couldn't possibly be something else, I almost didn't have the heart to tell him he was wrong.

"No, buddy, its not the gas, the gas is fine. I think it's the battery."

His brow furrowed as he considered this. "Hmm, the battery; sure, Daddy, that could be it."

I chuckled at him and climbed out of the car, Kyle still in the back seat, not knowing if he should exit the car with me. I waved for him to do just that and he opened the door and slid out, the wrestler still in his hand.

I began the process of elimination, trying to see if it was truly the battery. Overhead, three helicopters flew by, their rotors echoing off the rooftops.

Both Kyle and I watched them fly by, and when they had disappeared over the rooftops a few streets over, Kyle resumed playing and I got back to work. I opened the hood and did the usual stuff to try and figure out what was wrong with my baby, but after fifteen minutes of fussing under the hood, and my hands covered in grease, I gave up and slammed the hood hard. Behind me, Kyle jumped as he sat on the grass playing with his wrestler.

"Sorry, buddy," I said to him and he smiled and went back to the serious business of playing.

When I turned back around to face the car, Fred was smiling at me with one of his patented whole face grins.

"Hey, neighbor, having some car trouble?"

"Yeah, I am, I don't know, but I think the battery's dead."

"Oh? How old is it?"

I gave that some thought, trying to piece back the years when I had bought it. Kyle was two I think and that would mean the battery was going on five years, maybe a little more than that. I told Fred this and he nodded, like a surgeon being told the patient was going to die before he even attempted to operate.

"Well, there you go; it's probably time for a new one, anyway. Say, me and the guys were about to go to the market and hardware store. There's a Lappens on the way, we could stop by there on the way back if you want and you could get yourself a new one."

Lappens was the local automotive store.

"Oh yeah, you'd do that for me?" I asked him.

Fred moved closer and patted my shoulder in a grandfatherly way. "Of course I would, what are friends for?"

I gave that some thought and decided I was in a bind. I needed my car and Karen's was in the shop for at least another two days.

"Okay, Fred, I will come, and thanks again for the offer."

He waved as he turned away. "Not a problem, glad to help. Be at my jeep in ten minutes or miss the bus."

I told him fine, I'd be there and then dealt with closing up my car. With another weary sigh I took the keys from the ignition and locked the door. That seemed silly as the car wouldn't run even if I left my keys in the ignition, but old habits die hard.

"Hey, Kyle, you stay there and play and I'm gonna go inside for a sec' and tell your mom we're going with Fred. I'll be right back."

Kyle barely looked at me, too wrapped up in his action figure. "Sure, Daddy, 'kay."

I couldn't help but grin and feel that fatherly pride once again, then I climbed the back stairs and entered the house. Once Karen was informed I'd be leaving again, I'd already decided to take Kyle with me as I'd promised him a ride.

If only I'd known what a bad decision that would turn out to be.

4

THE RIDE TO THE STORE

WITH KYLE BY my side we walked down my driveway and took a right to Fred's house. His jeep was sitting in his driveway and Fred was leaning against the driver's side door, smoking a cigarette. I knew he was supposed to be quitting, so I didn't say anything.

Those cigarette butts had found their way onto my property far too many times over the years, the butts seeming to burrow into the grass. They drove me crazy. But other than that, Fred had been a good neighbor and I learned a long time ago that sometimes you need to let the little things pass.

Near Fred, also leaning on the side of the jeep, were three other men. One was Ted, and I couldn't repress the frown that came to my lips at seeing him. The other two were Bob Valentine and Carl Simmons, two other men who lived on my street. Carl was married to a fat, harpy of a wife and the two of them looked like an apple dating a stalk of celery. Carl was wickedly skinny, his thighs only a little larger than my arms and she was massively overweight and smoked like a chimney. When she walked, which wasn't far, she waddled back and forth like one of those weebles I played with as a kid. Sometimes I would see her when I picked Kyle up at school when I was home, wanting to give Karen a break, and she always got there early, sometimes a half hour or more, just so she could get one of the five or so parking spots in the front of the school.

Want to know my picture of Hell? How 'bout having sex with Carl's wife? The odor alone must be enough to kill the average man, not to mention with an ass so big just how exactly does she manage to wipe it? Yes, that was how big Carl's wife was. But despite all this, I always had to wonder what sex must be like for the two of them. I figured even if she was ugly as sin it must have been easy to screw her. If he was too tired to go for her vagina, I'll bet all he needed to do was push a couple of folds of fat together, add some olive oil, and there you go, instant vagina. Carl also had that rundown look of a man who knew his life was as good as it was going to get and I sometimes wondered if he might sit in his living room in the middle of the night with a gun barrel in his mouth while he decided whether to just end it and try again in the next life. In other words, the man was truly pathetic.

Carl was standing quite still, his hands in his pockets and I hoped a soft breeze didn't pop up and blow him away. He looked up from staring at his shoes and smiled wanly at me. I nodded in return and slowed when I reached Bob.

Where Carl was a skinny, scarecrow of a man, Bob was his polar opposite in every respect. Bob was six one with large biceps, and though he had a slight beer belly, the muscle surrounding it was rock hard. Bob had lifted weights when he was younger and even now, years later, the residue of that physique could still be seen. Bob was also married, but where Carl had an elephant for a wife, Bob had a gazelle. His wife, Sharon, was a statuesque blonde with all the right curves. Next to my wife, Sharon was one of the most beautiful women I had ever seen.

Bob was chewing on a matchstick and he said a quick hello to me. Bob and I weren't friends, but we weren't strangers either. We were the type of neighbors that would wave whenever we saw one another, but would never go that extra mile and actually talk. Once again, that was fine with me. I found out years ago to make your friends away from where you live, that way if there's ever a falling out, all you have to do is stop seeing them. Make friends with your neighbors, and if things go south, all you have to look forward to each day is dirty looks and mumblings when you see each other.

Before I was close enough to hear what Fred was saying, I already knew what the subject would be. Of course he was talking about the dark wall which seemed to swallow up New York and the surrounding countryside. Not that I could blame him. Whatever was happening was something so unreal it seemed like science fiction. But even though I was concerned, I was a little more grounded than Fred. I was in Massachusetts, after all, hundreds of miles away. What the hell could I do about it? As long as the wall stayed across the east coast, it was really none of my business.

Oh, sure, people will say how worried they are and how concerned they feel, but just like in a hurricane or a tsunami in another country, the problem is so far removed from the average American citizen to not really matter. Not that anyone would actually say that. No, we all have to act like we give a shit and send our best wishes when what we're really thinking is better you guys than us.

Fred stopped talking when he saw me and Kyle walking toward him and he smiled at us both.

"Hey, you guys, we've been waiting for you. Ready to go?"

I nodded and looked down at Kyle, who smiled halfheartedly. He was the only kid with four adult men and he had to feel slightly uncomfortable. I squeezed his shoulder and he looked up at me, eyes wide.

"You ready, sport?" I asked him. He nodded and we moved to the rear door while the other men climbed inside, as well.

Fred started the engine and pulled out of the driveway just as another helicopter flew by overhead.

"That's the fourth one in less than an hour," Fred said to no one in particular.

"Where the hell are they going?" Carl asked in his squeaky voice. He was the nerd every bully in high school dreamed of.

Fred only shrugged. "Probably nowhere. Whatever's happening in New York has got the entire U.S. of A. on alert."

"I think they're all dead in New York. Whatever that thing is, it blocks light and radio waves. For all we know it could block out the very air we breathe. New York's probably nothing but a graveyard," Bob commented from the passenger seat. He had moved for the shotgun position and I know I wasn't going to argue with him. Instead I had Kyle on my lap and Carl and Ted with me in the back seat. I didn't like Kyle not being in a seatbelt, but we were only three and a half miles away from the hardware store and supermarket and it was all side roads. With one exception.

We had to go through a rotary. Now, if you're not from New England, you may not know what a rotary is. A rotary is a large circle where vehicles go around and there are side entrances all around it. When someone comes from one of these side entrances, they have to slowly force their way into the circle and then slide out when they are at the next entrance they want. It would be a lot simpler to just have a four or five way intersection, but fifty years ago some architect high on crack, or something similar, had thought up the rotary. Massachusetts is one of the last states to actually use them. The French use them as well, but the less said about the French, the better.

"That's crazy," Ted said from across from me. "If they were all dead, surely we'd know that by now."

Bob turned slightly in his seat so he could look at Ted. "Oh yeah? Then why hasn't anyone driven out of the wall yet. There are thousands of people in there and no one has come out yet? No way, pal, they're all dead."

Kyle shifted uncomfortably in my lap and turned to look at me. His eyes were wide, but there was a little trepidation in there, as well. He looked like he wanted to cry, but was holding it back with all his might.

"Daddy, is that true? Are all the people dead in the dark wall? Is that going to happen to us, Daddy? Are we gonna die, too?"

"No, Kyle we certainly are not. We're fine here, don't worry, you're safe with me, right?"

He nodded slightly, but I really didn't know if he believed me or not.

"Hey, guys," I said, "how 'bout giving all the death stuff a rest, huh? You're scaring my son."

"Oh, shit, Johnny, sorry about that." Bob turned his gaze on Kyle. "Sorry, Kyle, I was just talking, I'm sure we're fine here."

I frowned slightly after hearing him call me Johnny. Bob always called me Johnny and I really hated it. It made me sound like I was five. But as Bob was twice my size and we weren't that close, I had never bothered to say anything about it.

"Hey, how about some music?" Fred asked. He had reached Broadway, the main thoroughfare of Revere and was waiting at the light to cross over to the east side of town.

No one objected and he turned on the radio. But instead of music, frazzled voices were talking about New York. Fred turned to me and smiled apologetically and began scanning the stations. All he found was talk, talk and more talk. Didn't surprise me in the least. This was big news. An entire state was hidden in some kind of darkness, almost like an eclipse, and no one knew why. The news would latch on to this for all it was worth. Even if the wall disappeared today, I knew I'd be hearing about it for months to come. Well, at least until the next news-worthy crisis occurred.

While we idled at the light, three police cruisers screamed by, their lights flashing in the late morning sun. It was almost noon by my watch, but there would be no quick screech of the siren because it was still on, filling the background of our world with noise. But we were closer to the fire station now and the siren was louder. Fred had the windows closed or I believe it would have been loud enough to inhibit talking.

The light changed to green and Fred moved on, passing the shops and banks that lined the sidewalks. People were out and about, proving my theory that even though people act like they care, they only worry about themselves in the end.

Fred finally gave up and left the radio on one of the chattering stations. A man and women were going on and on about the strange occurrence and everyone in the jeep was quiet as they listened. Kyle stared out the window, entertained by the people. He still had his wrestler, which I hadn't known when he had boarded the jeep, and he played with it idly.

The last leg of the journey came five minutes later when we approached the rotary. Fred approached it from a side street and he was supposed to yield, waiting for his turn to enter. But whether he was an aggressive driver or just too damn old, he drove right into the circle, cutting off three cars and a motorcycle. My heart was in my throat as I stared at the front grilles of the oncoming cars, but then the jeep was in the circle and moving around it. Honks and yells, and a few choice imprecations floated on the wind, but if Fred heard them, he didn't let on. My heart was beating fast and I sure wished Kyle had on a seatbelt now. If I had known Fred drove as bad as most people his age, I may have rethought this whole trip.

"Uhm, Fred, I think you were supposed to yield back there," I said as I breathed out a long sigh. I had a habit of doing that when dealing with things beyond my control.

"Really? Naw, I was fine. I had plenty of room," Fred answered back.

"Yeah, if you were an ant. That was somethin' else, Fred. I'm glad I'm not your insurance carrier," Ted said from next to me. Fred made a face that only an old man can make, with his jaw set and his nose turned to the side, but he remained silent. I looked at Ted and he grinned, knowing what I meant.

Bob said nothing and Carl seemed to be in his own world as we finished the rest of the journey in relative silence. Actually, everyone wanted to hear the radio, and I had to admit, so did I. Whatever was happening in New York was chillingly scary and I prayed it would stay away from us and the rest of America. With this crisis growing, I already was imagining the gas prices going up yet again. Nowadays, it seems like if a butterfly farts too loudly in the wind it's an excuse for gas prices to go up at the pumps.

Fred turned down a side street and headed for the beach, which was where the supermarket and hardware store was located. When you were standing in front of the supermarket, the beach was less than four blocks away.

When Fred reached the entrance to the Stop & Shop and pulled into the parking lot, all our jaws fell open at the sight before us. The lot was packed, people running back and forth to their cars with carts full of groceries. Screaming kids were pulled along by weary mothers and it seemed we weren't the only ones with the idea to go to the store and stock up.

Fred continued on and found a parking spot far away from the entrance to the store.

"Well, we better get in there before they run out of stuff," Fred suggested. We all nodded, and one at a time climbed out of the jeep. We each grabbed a cart and headed for the doors of the supermarket. Kyle was in my carriage, sitting with his head perked up as he watched the activity around him.

"It's a good thing no one's panicking," Bob said sarcastically as he pushed his cart around a squished banana on the ground.

"Yeah, if not, this place might be crazy," Ted added in the same tone while he followed.

With people moving about, cars pulling in and out of spaces, horns blaring when people didn't move fast enough, our little group headed inside the store.

5

THE SUPERMARKET AND THE HIGH PRICE FOR MILK

THE HARDWARE STORE

MICHELLE'S TIGHT SHIRT

DARKNESS FALLS

THE GLASS DOOR opened when Fred stepped on the magnetic platform, the rest of us following him. With the first step inside the supermarket, all four of us couldn't help but stop and try to take in the chaos in front of us. Every checkout aisle was full, people desperately trying to buy whatever they could. I found it not surprising in the least. Why was it that whenever something was happening in the world, there were always people who immediately turned into squirrels, trying to pack as much supplies away as they could?

"Holy shit, will you look at this?" Bob said while he stared with his mouth open. We all joined him and only moved when we were pushed aside like chattel as more people swarmed into the store.

I couldn't believe how crowded the store was. It was like a Toys R Us the morning after Thanksgiving. The large aisle behind the checkout counters was full to capacity. If I had to guess, I'd say we would be in line for over an hour, maybe more. We all walked into the store, studying the faces of the people around us. Everyone had a manic look, like the world was about to come to an end and they needed to make sure they had enough toilet paper and mouthwash to usher them into the next world.

I mean, it was outrageous what some people had in their carriages. I saw one woman with ten bottles of Soy sauce, three bottles of ketchup and one of mustard, the spicy kind, not the yellow. I had an irresistible urge to go find a package of hot dogs and toss it into her carriage just so she would have at least a few things that made sense. Another person in line, a balding man with a big nose, had five Duraflame logs and a bushel of fresh picked corn, not shucked, probably because he had no time to do it in the store.

It was absolute madness.

But still we wandered deeper into the store, not a little because we were being pushed by others behind us. It was like we were in a river with the current steadily pushing us farther downstream. Kyle cried out, scared of all the noise and I decided the carriage was useless as I could barely move with it. The instant I took Kyle out of it, it was snatched up by a woman with three children. All three kids had dirty faces and runny noses and I heard the mom yell at them to hold onto the carriage. I had a feeling if one let go, the kid would be washed away in a sea of humanity to be found later when things calmed down. I wished the kids well and tried to get out of the way of the flowing carriages. The noise was deafening. The beeps of the registers and the yelling of the customers reminded me what it was like to go to Fanueil Hall on the weekend. Try to get through there and all you'll get for your trouble is an elbow in the ribs about three dozen times.

"Daddy, I'm scared, I want to go home," Kyle said and buried his face in my chest.

"We will, sport, just give me another minute or so," I told him. He nodded and burrowed deeper into my shirt.

We were still near the first checkout line and I began to hear someone yelling over the voices of the others. I turned my head to find the voice and saw it was a man in line at the checkout. He was the one who was being helped by the cashier, an exhausted looking teenager, and he was arguing about the three gallons of milk he'd purchased. The manager arrived, and as I listened, I heard the manager begin to yell back, stating that milk had gone up in the present crisis and it was now five dollars a gallon. The man wasn't happy about that, and after a few more back and forths, the man jumped over the counter and attacked the manager. Other people gathered around, cheering for the customer and it took almost three minutes before two policemen charged into the fray and broke it up. Both cops looked exhausted and didn't seem to care what had happened or who had started it. I was going to keep watching when I felt someone tug on my shirt sleeve. It was Fred and he was shaking his head back and forth like a bobble head.

"This is crazy, John. I think maybe we should just get out of here, unless there's some stuff you really, really need."

I couldn't help but chuckle at that, thinking of the list from Karen in my back pocket. "Fred, there's nothing I need this bad, I'm with you. Let's get the hell out of here."

Next to Fred were Bob, Carl and Ted who were still watching the crowds, and after a few words were exchanged between Fred and the two men, all four of us began the odyssey of trying to leave the store. At first, it didn't look like we were going to be able to get out. There was a line of people blocking the exits and there were simply just too many people to try to pass through. But then Bob moved up to the point man's position and began elbowing people out of the way.

A man was shoved and he turned around abruptly, anger in his eyes.

"Hey, what the hell? I oughta..." he stopped in mid-sentence when he looked up at Bob.

"You oughta what?" Bob asked, glaring down at the smaller man.

"Nothing, mister, nothing at all. Would you excuse me?" He asked and then slinked back into the crowd. Bob grinned as the man dissolved into thin air and then turned to us and waved us forward. With Bob in the lead like a snowplow, it didn't take long to escape the supermarket and back into the fresh air of the summer's day. We all moved against the brick facing of the building and breathed a great sigh of relief while harried men and women ran past us.

"Jesus, what the hell is wrong with those people?" Ted asked as he moved his head back and forth like he was watching a game of tennis. He just couldn't stop watching the people running in and out of the supermarket.

"Panicking, that's what's wrong with them. There's nothing they can do but wait and some people can't take that," Fred suggested as he began moving away from the supermarket's doors and back to the parking lot. Just as he stepped into the road, he was almost run down by a crazy driver. Only Bob's quick reflexes saved Fred from being run down as he grabbed him by the arm and yanked him back to the curb. A horn blasted as the vehicle drove by and Fred breathed out a loud gasp.

"Wow, thank you, Bob, that was a close one."

"Well, just pay more attention, will ya? I won't always be around to save your wrinkled hide."

We all shared a chuckle at that, and when it was clear again, crossed the parking lot and climbed back into Fred's jeep.

Without delay, Fred turned over the engine and pulled out. No sooner had he backed out of his space than a small SUV filled it. Fred payed it no mind, but pulled down the row of cars and back onto the main road. This took almost ten minutes as we waited for the line of vehicles to move. Once on the road again, Fred pointed the jeep towards the hardware store. It was only a minute down the road and we got there in five, the traffic still heavy because of the supermarket. Fred found a space a few car lengths from the front doors of the hardware store. It was when I realized it was a handicapped spot and was about to say something when Fred pulled out the placard from his glove box and hung it on the rearview mirror.

"There we go, guys; sometime it pays to get old, though there's not much else to look forward to."

With a few chuckles, Carl barely acknowledging the joke at all, we all climbed out and headed for the hardware store, hoping at least here there would be a little less insanity. Kyle held on tight to me, not wanting to let go after the chaos of the supermarket. I didn't blame him one bit.

My eyes played over the front of the hardware store. Signs in the window proclaimed trash barrels for $8.99 and potting soil for three for ten dollars. Near the doors, a few old posters still hung, some worn and faded from the sun, the tape used to fasten them to the glass aged a light yellow.

The words True Value was printed on the glass across the double doors and below that the words: Stern's Hardware. Add that to the big red sign connected to the top of the building's façade and anyone who could read knew what this particular building was used for.

Not that it was needed.

Everyone in Revere knew where Sterns was located. It was a regular landmark. If you needed to give someone directions to the beach, you would tell them to go to Sterns and then take a left at the light. Then go straight and you'll see the water. I'd done this myself on multiple occasions and I have to assume the people got there because later when I went by, I never saw the same people wandering around clueless.

I noticed a gray work van with the picture of a cockroach and a spider dancing together in comical form painted on the side of it, and a second later spotted a man with a baseball cap and large tank on his back, holding some kind of sprayer in his hand. He was walking around the hardware store spraying the walls and foundation. The man continued on and soon was lost behind the building and I forgot about him.

We slowed as we approached the double doors. There were four unruly looking men hanging about in the front of the building. All were dark skinned, each one looking rough and impetuous; but that wasn't what made them look truly threatening. It was the red bandanas they all wore on their arms and the tattoos crisscrossing their arms and necks. Now, I don't know much about gangs and the like, but I think I've watched enough television and movies to know what gangbangers look like.

Fred was in the lead as always and he slowed when he approached the first man in front of the store.

"Whatchoo lookin' at, old man?" The gangbanger asked. No wait, demanded would be a better description of his tone. He had solid, metal covered teeth, what I think they call a grille. His tattoos covered both his arms, his hair was done up in cornrows and I think there was a bulge under his shirt just above the waistband of his pants. I swallowed hard, thinking it must be a gun. Looking over my shoulder, there was no sign of a police presence and probably wouldn't be for the time being. It seemed the city was falling apart as people panicked about something happening three states over.

It was Bob who saved the day again, moving in front of Fred and looking down at the black man. Bob was almost a foot taller than the gangbanger, and when he stood to his full height, he might have added another inch or two.

"Look, guys, we don't want no trouble. Just move aside and we'll be out of your way," Bob said with a grin that said the exact opposite.

"Damn, will you look at this cracker? Think he's all that and shit," one of the other gangbangers said. This man was overweight and had curly black hair with a gold earring in each of his ears. When he smiled, there were at least three gold teeth.

I was starting to get scared. These guys looked bad, and though I could defend myself if needed, I was well past my high school days of brawling in the school yard. Plus, I had Kyle to watch out for and a fight with these men would accomplish nothing. Not to mention we were outnumbered. Fred was an old man and Carl would be useless. I glanced askance to see him and he looked like he wanted to curl up and die. Ted at least was standing tall. My respect for him went up a notch. Behind us, a police siren split the day, overriding that damn siren from the fire station. When the siren of the police car sounded, all four black men seemed to look up, like deer caught in the headlights of an approaching car. Then they parted like the Red Sea, not wanting trouble with the police. Neither Bob nor the rest of us paused to assess the situation, but instead moved into the hardware store. We would worry about leaving when it was time to go. I knew I needed some candles, batteries, and maybe another flashlight, so I definitely wanted to get in the hardware store.

One at a time we moved through the glass doors, with me going in first, Carl cringing when he walked by the gangbangers. One of them barked at Carl like a dog and Carl jumped, then ran by me like a frightened child. I shook my head and followed him inside.

When the glass doors swung shut, the siren faded to dull background noise again and I looked up at the five old men standing around the counter.

"Well, I'll be, if it isn't little Johnny Russell," the older man behind the counter said in a rusty voice filled with age, and a wide smile across his weathered face. This was the owner of the hardware store and had been the sole proprietor for over fifty years. So far, Norman Sterns had even managed to stay open with the threat of a Home Depot coming to Chelsea, which was only a mile or so away from his building.

"Hi ya, Mr. Sterns, how ya been?" I asked.

Mr. Sterns shrugged. "Fair to midland, Johnny, that's' about it." He looked up when Fred walked in and an even larger smile creased his lips, showing off his dentures. "And is that Fred Harper? You old dog, where the hell have you been? I haven't seen you in weeks."

"Hey there yourself, Norman. Sorry I haven't been by, but the wife's been sick and I've been busy."

My eyebrows went up at that statement. I hadn't really given it much thought, but now that I thought about it, I hadn't seen Fred's wife around as much as before. When I had seen her this morning, she did look rather pale, as if she wasn't getting enough sleep. Usually I'd see her on her front porch fiddling with her flowers, but this year the flowers were dead and hadn't been attended to at all. I had thought I'd known everything I needed to know about my neighbor and I just found something else that was entirely new. Goes to show you that people can fool you if they want to.

"Sorry, to hear that, Fred, Margie's a wonderful gal."

"Yes, she is, thanks for that," Fred said and then changed the subject when he saw the small television set on the counter behind Norman. Pictures of the dark wall were on it and a news reporter was prattling on. "How 'bout that shit, crazy huh?"

Norman nodded, as did the other men. I recognized two of them from past visits to the hardware store. One was Earl and the other was Edward, but his friends called him Buddy for short. Where you get Buddy from Edward I have no idea, but maybe it was a middle name or nickname. I nodded to each of them in succession; the other two men ignored me. They were all sitting on stools that resemble what you'd find in a bar. All they needed were beers and cigarettes in each hand to make the picture complete.

"You're just in time to watch, Fred," Norman said and also made eye contact with me, Bob, Carl and Ted. "They're about to do some kind of experiment to that wall." He shook his head back and forth. "It's unbelievable, whatever it is." The other men all nodded, agreeing with their leader.

Fred moved closer to the counter so he could see the small twelve inch black and white television better. The picture was blurry, thanks to the reception. No cable here, just old fashioned rabbit ears. I followed him, curious, as well. Kyle shifted in my arms and I repositioned him. Times like this was when I realized how big he was getting, or how old I was becoming.

"So what's up? What're they gonna do?" Bob asked as he stared at the men and the television. He towered over all of us, like a Greek god coming down from Olympus to hang with us mortals. I thought of my checker game with Kyle and chuckled. Luckily no one heard me so I didn't have to explain myself.

Norman gestured to the television. "Seems some scientist types want to send in some kind of pulse generator or something. Says it has enough power to light a city. Figure that should shed some light on whatever that damn thing is."

"Think it'll work?" Ted asked from the side of the group. He was trying to see everything at once. We weren't the only people in the store. There were about a half dozen people, a mix of men and women, also buying emergency supplies. A pimple faced teenager was at the only register, ringing items up as fast as he could. Norman didn't seem to care. He did notice Ted looking at the teenager and gestured to the kid.

"That's my grandson, Willy. He works here on weekends and in the summer. I got him for another month before school starts back up."

Ted nodded. "He seems like he's overloaded over there. There's a lot of people in line."

"Yeah, there is, but he'll do fine. An extra second ain't gonna kill anyone." As if on cue, the peanut gallery all agreed. Norman was the head man and the other four were his followers. They were like children hanging out after school; only instead of a clubhouse they had the hardware store. I couldn't help but look for the sign that read, No Girls Allowed scrawled in crayon somewhere nearby.

"So what's up with those guys outside the store?" I asked. "They made it tough to come in here."

Norman nodded, scowling heavily. "Yeah, don't I know it. Those assholes have been here for almost two hours. I told them to get away from my store, but they told me it's a free country and flipped me off. I called the police, but they say they're too busy for something as trivial as that. But don't you worry, about them," he said and turned to pick up a heavy twelve-gauge shotgun with a polished wooden stock. "They won't be bothering us for much longer."

"Why, what are you gonna do, Norm, shoot them? Shit, this isn't the Old West, you know." Fred said this. He did it with a chuckle in his voice, but he was more than a little serious.

"Maybe not, Fred, but a man has the right to protect his property. I'm just giving them a chance to leave on their own."

I didn't think those gangbangers would be leaving anytime soon, but I kept my mouth shut. Really, it was none of my business. Besides, I had to think of Kyle first.

The doors opened and the man with the tank on his back strolled inside and walked over to the counter. He smiled politely enough at each of us standing around the counter.

"All rightie, folks, the entire buildings sprayed. Give it a day or two to take the most effect, but you ought to see results in less than an hour."

He handed Norman an invoice and smiled broadly. "You can pay that anytime, Mr. Sterns. Check or a credit card number will be fine."

Norman took the invoice, studied the numbers and then slid the invoice into his pocket.

"Thanks, Bill, hopefully this'll settle the problem," he gave Bill a look that said they were through.

Bill nodded. "I'm sure it will, but if you don't like the results, give me another call and I'll come back again with some stronger stuff." He glanced at each of us again. "Well, I've got to go, more people to see and bugs to kill."

Norman waved the man away and a few of us said bye to this complete stranger.

"What's with the exterminator?" Fred asked curious.

Norman scowled, his wrinkles growing, making him look like an old prune.

"Ah, it's nothing big. Saw some roaches and mice and shit the other day in the back. They come in with the fertilizer I'm told. So I had a guy come and spray for bugs, that's all." He shook his head and scowled deeply. "Bugs, I hate the damn critters."

"Hey, they're gonna start the test," Earl said, his nasally voice sounding like he was a cancer patient. As if on cue, the man did light a cigarette, blowing the smoke straight up into the air so it wouldn't bother anyone. The law now said there was no smoking in public businesses, but at the moment there wasn't exactly anyone around to enforce the law and Norman didn't seem to mind one bit. A woman came up and asked Norman where the shovels were and I casually turned to see who the woman might be, thinking the voice sounded familiar.

My jaw fell open when I realized I knew this woman.

"Michelle? Michelle Bennett? Is that you?" I asked as I looked into the woman's eyes.

She turned to look at me and her blue eyes lit up with recognition. "John? John Russell? Oh my God, what a surprise? What are you doing here and who is this?" She was now looking directly at Kyle who still had his head buried in my chest. He was shy and there were so many new faces it was probably overwhelming for him.

"This is my son, Kyle," I told her.

"Oh, wow, he's so cute. So you're married?"

I nodded and waved my right hand so she could see the ring. "Yeah, almost ten years this winter. You?"

She shook her head no. "No, never found the right guy. Well, I did once, but I let him get away." Her eyes seemed to grow steamy and I found myself growing warm. Michelle and I had a past. Just before I met Karen, I had been seeing Michelle. We had been a really good pair until she had decided to go to college out of state. I decided those long distant relationships rarely work, so we had split up. She left the state and I stayed. End of story. But sometimes, late at night, I wonder about what might have been. If she had stayed in Massachusetts, I have no doubt we would have gotten married and settled down together. But like so many other people in the world, it didn't do any good to ponder the road not taken.

I didn't know what to say to her and luckily I was spared a retort. While we looked at each other, Michelle waiting for me to answer, Norman called to anyone around the counter that the television was about to show what the scientists were doing. Thankfully, she turned away, curious as to what Norman was going on about. We all moved closer to the counter, the two old farts I didn't know frowning slightly as we encroached on their territory. Bob moved next to me and his eyes drifted over Michelle's body, his eyes hovering at her chest. Michelle was still very beautiful with long blonde hair and smooth skin and I had to admit I was admiring her breasts as they moved about in her tight t-shirt. Her deep blue eyes were still the same and I realized I could just as easily fall into them now as I had ten years ago. She looked up at Bob and he smiled back at her, flexing his muscles in his tight t-shirt. She smiled back politely, but other than that wasn't impressed by him. After a few seconds went by, Bob got the hint and he slouched slightly, but then his attention was focused on the television.

We all stood at the counter in the hardware store as a large flatbed truck backed up to the massive dark wall. There were three men with white containment suits standing next to a large square, metal box on the rear platform. They played with a few gears and knobs as a reporter did a voice over and the sides of the box opened and white discs that seemed like radar dishes popped out. The reporter droned on. All the guy was doing was telling us, the viewers, what we were seeing. He was needed as much as a lead weight would be to a drowning man, but that was the news.

Two minutes went by and one of the scientists stood tall and gave the thumbs up to someone off the screen. All three men quickly climbed off the platform and the truck began to back up as the dishes began to power up, taking on a dull glow that was growing with each passing second. It was eerie the way the rear of the truck and the square machine were swallowed up by the darkness like it was quicksand.

Everyone was quiet, even the reporter, as we all watched with baited breath. When the truck had backed up until only the cab was still visible, the driver hopped out and ran for his life. I didn't blame him much.

Seconds ticked by and nothing happened, but then the truck seemed to move on its own. Everyone around it jumped as the tires seemed to be moving back and forth as if there was something in the dark that was pushing it and then letting go.

All of a sudden, the cab of the truck was sucked into the dark wall, and perhaps it was my imagination, but it looked like the front tires of the truck never rolled. It was like the truck had been picked up an inch off the ground and then yanked into the darkness like it was nothing more than a feather.

With jaws agape, we all watched in fear as a bright burst of light filled the center of the dark wall right where the truck had disappeared. Then nothing. No one spoke, and I knew I was waiting with fear in my chest for what might happen next. I got my wish, but not the way I might have wanted it.

Looking back now, I believe the next events happened one at a time incredibly close together, but at the time it seemed like everything happened at once. The first thing to happen was the television screen went dark. At first we thought it was the set, but when the channel was changed, we still got other channels. After a few moments of flipping channels, Norman was at the idea that something had happened in New York. As weird as it sounds, every single television crew that had been broadcasting from the wall was missing. No one was broadcasting and the news anchors back at the stations were baffled. Now, only seconds had gone by since the screen had gone dark and then, to everyone's surprise, the power went out in the hardware store. At first no one panicked and Norman thought it might have been a fuse, but when his grandson went to the double doors and looked outside, he saw the traffic lights were out, as well.

Before the next decision could be made, there came the sounds of crashing vehicles and hundreds of people screaming.

"What the hell is that?" Bob asked as he looked to the front doors.

"That sounds like it's coming from the beach," Norman said while he looked out one of the plate glass windows that lined the front of the store. It was then I noticed the siren from the fire station, the one that had been sounding continually since I had gotten up that morning. It was finally silent.

More screams filled the air and we all looked at one another. Bob was the first to the double doors, wanting to investigate. "I'm going to the beach, anyone want to come with me?"

I wanted to go as well, but I had Kyle with me. The beach was a block and a half away and Kyle would be quite a burden to carry. Michelle saw my face as I looked at Bob and then down at my son, and she held out her hands.

"Go 'head if you want, I'll watch him for you."

"Thanks," I said and handed Kyle over to her. He fussed and I told him she was a friend and he would be safe with her. At first he didn't want to, but then he relented.

"Come on, already, I want to go," Bob called, he couldn't wait to see what the problem was, like a car crash you pass and you look to see if anyone's hurt, but he didn't want to go alone.

"I'll be right back, champ, you'll be fine," I told Kyle, and then, with Ted by my side, we all left the hardware store.

The moment we stepped outside, the yelling and screaming was five times as loud, and it was all coming from the beach.

With Bob in the lead, we all took off down the sidewalk, passing the four gangbangers as we went. One of them gave Bob a dirty look, but they let us pass. We moved at a steady gait, more of a jog really, and in no time we were at the rise on the street that would take you right into the large sidewalk that lined a section of the beach. Revere Beach was about a mile and a half long, maybe two, and it spanned from Winthrop to Swampscott and beyond.

Normally the view was beautiful. With the water and the waves going off into the horizon and the few boats that were always in the distance floating like a child's toy in a bathtub. To the left was Swampscott and there were a few attractive buildings to daydream at and of course the beach itself, usually filled with beachgoers, some wearing small to nothing for bathing suits. On any given day the beach would have been filled with children playing in the water, people flying kites or playing soccer, and the others who were just laying out as their skin slowly collected the rays that would one day give them skin cancer.

But not today.

Today the beach was chaos as people ran about, knocking one another over while they tried desperately to get to their cars and get away from the black death that was heading for them, because where the water and clear blue sky would normally be, should have been, there was nothing but a massive wall of darkness that spanned as far left and right as I could see and as high as I could look up. An airplane was coming into Logan Airport and I watched the airplane fly into the wall of darkness. What happened to it after that I never found out. Even the roar of the turbines, when the pilot tried to veer away at the last second, ceased the instant the aircraft entered the wall.

People were running past us, towels in their hands as they ran for their lives. Bob, Ted and I all had to move to the side of the sidewalk or risk getting trampled.

"Jesus Christ, will you look at that," Bob said in a hoarse voice. His eyes were so wide they looked like they would pop out of his head. I felt the same way, a fear so unimaginable I couldn't contemplate it filling my stomach. There was actually only one other time when I felt a fear like this. I was nine or ten and I was playing on the railroad tracks behind my house in Malden. Me and two friends were running in the high weeds that lined the edge of the railroad tracks. Well, one of my friends found a rat and we began chasing it along the tracks. Eventually, we managed to corner it in a copse of shrubs and I found out the hard way what happens when you do that to a wild animal. The rat actually leaped off the ground and went right for my throat, and by the luck of God or another saint watching over me, I moved my arm in front of my body out of instinct. The rat's incisors sank into my left wrist instead of my neck and I shrieked in pain and fright as I waved my arm around me. The rat never let go, its teeth in good and deep and that same luck finally came to my aid when the rat let go on its own accord. It darted off into the weeds and I looked at the two bleeding holes in my wrist. With my friend's help, and weak knees, I made it home where I went to the hospital to get checked out. Luckily I didn't get rabies. But I'll never forget the terror I felt as that rat dangled from my arm with my blood flicking away like raindrops.

That terror was back now as I stared at the massive wall of darkness. It was like the world simply ended, and if you went to that wall, you would merely fall off into space.

"Holy shit, it's moving!" Ted yelled and pointed at the wall. "And it's moving fast!"

I followed his gaze and realized he was right. If you looked at the wall and where it touched the ocean's surface and compared it to the shoreline it was obvious it was still moving, absorbing the ocean and heading straight for us at a good clip. If we were stupid enough to stay where we were, we would be inside that darkness in less than a minute.

Three helicopters soared overhead and I looked up as they flew by, their rotors dampening the sounds of the yelling people around us. More crashing cars and trucks could be heard as the beach strip became gridlock. A few explosions entered the mix and I wondered what could have caused them.

But then it went silent as the darkness flooded over the boardwalk and silenced the people and cars forever.

"Oh my God, oh shit," Ted mumbled and made the sign of the cross on his chest.

"Come on, guys, we need to get back to the store and tell them what's happening, right now," I said as I began to move backward. It was hard looking away. It was like looking at something God would do if he was so inclined to, it was that amazing.

"Damn straight," Bob said and turned and began running with the fleeing beach goers. We ran now, not jogged, back to the hardware store and in no time were back at the double doors. I glanced behind me and a scream filled my mouth as I saw the dark wall was only a hundred feet behind me.

"Hurry up, its right behind us!" I yelled. My heart was trip-hammering in my chest, I was so terrified. I kept waiting for the darkness to envelop me and then, well, I had no idea what would happen then and I didn't want to know.

The four gangbangers were running alongside us, but they were in no mood for a fight as they were running for their lives, as well. When we turned away from them and headed for the hardware store, the one with the metal teeth turned also, calling his three friends to follow. Upon reaching the doors, I threw them open, and Ted and Bob followed me inside. Then the four gangbangers came in, sneakers slapping the tiles and heavy gasps for breath filling the air as we all tried to catch our breaths after our dash back to the store. The gangbangers moved past us into the shadows of the store and went into the far aisle to be lost from sight. I don't think anyone even noticed them come in, as all eyes were on me, Ted and Bob.

Fred turned as we charged inside and his face was covered with curiosity. "What are you guys doing? Why are you out of breath? What'd you see?"

Before any of us could answer, the darkness enveloped the hardware store and the sun disappeared like it had been plucked out of the sky. Not knowing what to do, I ran for Kyle and Michelle and wrapped my hands around them both, thinking of Karen at the same time. Was that wall of darkness going to continue right to my house or was it going to stop? I didn't know and could only pray she was all right and would be smart if it did happen. All around me, people were talking, yelling and a few were screaming. Only the small backup lights Norman had on the walls, connected to batteries in the back room, illuminated the store, and as we all stood around in the almost pitch-black darkness, Bob turned and moved back to the glass double doors. He peered outside, trying to see anything, but there was nothing to see. It was utter blackness, like God had laid a giant tarp over the earth to block out the light.

"Anything out there?" Norman called to Bob while he rustled up some candles from behind the counter. He handed two of the old men a flashlight each.

Bob shook his head no. "There's nothing but darkness. What the hell is going on? Where the hell did the sun go?"

Before anyone could answer or even make a suggestion, the first of the creatures we would encounter crashed into the double doors and tried to enter the hardware store. I truly believe if Bob hadn't been standing there, and managed to close the doors and turn the lock, things might have started out very differently. But he was there, and he did keep the doors closed. The creature bounced off the glass and disappeared as fast as it had appeared, and no one, not even Bob, was able to get a good look at it.

"What the fuck was that?" Bob screamed as he jumped away from the door. There was a small slime trail on the door left from whatever had smacked it.

No one could answer him, as Bob had been the only one to even come close to seeing it. Most of us just assumed it had been a dog or something similar.

With the doors locked up, we all tried to settle down and get control of ourselves as the darkness surrounded us like a cloak of death. Not knowing what to do, I held Kyle and squeezed him tight and stared out the front plate-glass windows to where the parking lot used to be. I kept waiting for more people to bang on the doors to be let in, but no one came.

Next to me, Michelle was shaking with fear, so I held out my free hand to her. Taking it, she moved closer to me, and the three of us didn't move as around us the others began debating what was happening and what had happened to the sun. The other half dozen customers who had been in the store at the time joined the rest of us at the counter and began talking, filling the store with their voices.

While they argued with each other, another question came to me, as well. When we had entered the hardware store just before the dark enveloped us, there had been hundreds of people out on the street. So if that was true, then how come the instant the darkness descended every scream was silenced? I had a feeling I didn't want my question answered, so I didn't bring it up. Instead, I slid down to the floor, my back against the counter and held Kyle as tightly as I could, as if by doing this fatherly gesture, I could somehow make things better.

6

COOPERATION

FOUR MORE JOIN THE GROUP

FOR THE NEXT fifteen minutes, the people around me argued.

Back and forth each voice would go, suggesting what they thought was happening, and then their voice would be squelched by someone else yelling louder than them.

I sat on the floor with Kyle and Michelle and let everyone yell it out. I studied the new faces around me while everyone tried their best to place some normalcy to an abnormal situation.

There was an older woman in her seventies with her gray hair done up in a coquettish bun and wire rimmed glasses hanging from a chain on her chest. She had that grandmotherly look that allowed her to wear these glasses on the chain. Only a certain kind of elderly woman was able to pull this look off and she did it with taste and class. Later that day, I found out her name was Judith Mahoney and she was a widow of almost ten years. She was an opinionated woman who didn't take lightly to someone else telling her what to do. Even with her wrinkles and gray hair, the architecture of her face still showed me the beautiful young woman she had once been in her twenties.

Next to Judith Mahoney was a man about my age with dark brown hair which was cut close to his head and small eyes. He wore a windbreaker, despite the fact it was a little warm for one. By listening to him talk, I found out his name was George Lipton and he lived only a few blocks from the hardware store. His wife and kids were home alone and he was very worried about them. If I had seen George on the street on any given day, I would have thought he might have been a plain-clothed policeman, he just had that look about him.

The other four customers who were in the store were a mystery to me at the moment. The entire time I'd been in the hardware store, I never got the names of the young couple in their twenties. I'm sure they were married, as they clung to each other like glue, and one time I saw the flash of a ring on the young woman's left hand where a wedding ring should be. The other two people were average looking guys in their mid-thirties. They hovered together near the edge of the light from Norman's candle and never went far away from one another. I had a small feeling the two might have been gay, though I couldn't put my finger on any one reason why I thought this.

So far, everyone's arguing was doing nothing more than aggravating others who didn't like what they were hearing. Bob almost came to blows with one of the older men I didn't know personally, and it was only Ted who managed to stop the altercation by talking some sense into Bob and calming him down. I had to give the old man credit for sticking up for himself. I had to assume he wasn't bright enough to know this wasn't the time for posturing.

In a world of civilization, Bob couldn't touch the older man for fear of repercussions, but at the moment they were all alone and it was possible new rules would apply, such as only the strong should survive.

Angry from the argument, Bob had walked away to stand by the double-glass doors again. His eyes strained to pierce the blackness surrounding the outside of the store, but if he saw anything, he didn't inform the rest of us.

Finally, it was Fred who took charge and regained some semblance of order.

"All right, all ready, quiet, everybody!" He screamed loudly as he stood on a step stool from aisle four. "Now, listen up; we need to calm down and figure this thing out rationally. Whatever is happening, at least we're safe for the moment. Once we have a plan, we can figure out our next move."

"Next move? There is no next move. We're screwed," that came from one of the gay guys.

"Now that kind of talk isn't productive and I'd appreciate it if anyone who feels like that would keep it to himself," Fred replied back, quieting the man down. Fred turned to look at Norman who looked like a ghoul in the flickering candlelight. "Norman, we need to get as much light in here as we can. Can you get all the flashlights and batteries from the store and pile them up here?"

"Well, yeah, I could, but who's gonna pay for all that stuff?"

Fred made a face like he was talking to an idiot. "Tell you what, Norman, I will, I'll pay for it all. Just run a tab if you want to. If we make it out of here alive, then I'll pay you whatever you want, all right?"

Norman gave that some thought and then nodded. "All right, fine, as long as someone's paying for it, I'll get you whatever you need." He called Willy, his grandson, over to him and the frightened teenager moved from the shadows into the wan illumination of the candle. "Willy, go get everything Fred here just said and make it quick. Oh, and get those oil lanterns from aisle five." He handed the boy a small penlight so he could see where he was going. Hesitantly, with a shaking hand, Willy took the flashlight and moved off into the hardware store to be lost in the shadows of the aisles. He returned a second later, grabbed one of the few shopping carts near the front of the store and then moved off again, the wheels of the cart screeching slightly.

"Okay, that's good," Fred said. "The next thing we need to do is decide if we're going to stay here or leave and get back to our homes."

George stepped up and nodded then. "That's a good idea. I've got a family at home and I know my wife must be scared out of her mind. I'm for that. I need to get home to my family. It's just dark outside, so why are we all standing around? Let's get out of here," he said, repeating himself.

Fred held his hands up to calm George down.

"Now, just hold on a minute, there, mister, let's not go and do something you might regret. We don't know what has truly happened and it would be foolish to just go out there without knowing all the facts. My wife is home alone, too, and I want to get to her as soon as possible, but a few more minutes won't change a thing."

"Yeah, me too. My baby's home alone and I want to get back to her, too, but not before I know it's safe," Bob added.

George shook his head, the fear in his eyes apparent even in the dull lighting. "I don't care what you think, you old bastard, my family needs me and I'm leaving right now!" He snapped at Fred.

He probably would have, too, but something happened that caused him to pause. Out of the darkness, at the rear of the store, four more bodies approached the counter, and as I watched from the side, I knew who they were before the first face was visible. The metal teeth reflected whatever dim light they touched and I knew it was the gangbanger from the front of the hardware store when I had entered less than an hour ago, but already felt like days.

Norman reacted first, bringing the shotgun he stored behind the counter level with the top of the Formica and pumped the weapon.

"What the fuck are you people doing in my store?" He asked with a growl, the threat in his voice all too obvious.

The man with the metal teeth slowly raised his hands in front of him and smiled almost casually. Even in the gloom of the store, I noticed the smile didn't reach the man's eyes.

"Now, just hold on there, Grandpa, we're not gonna give you any trouble. We just ran in here when all that dark shit fell down around us out there. Now just be cool and no one will get hurt."

Three of the gangbangers moved a little closer, the other one hanging back, and I wondered if they were all crazy. They were standing in front of a man with a loaded shotgun and they didn't seem fazed in the least.

Norman flashed Metal Face another scowl. "Seems the only one's who are gonna get hurt is you and your homies."

Metal Face chuckled at that. I didn't blame him. Hearing Norman use a word like homies was rather comical.

"Actually, man, if you don't put that gun down right now, I think someone else might get hurt," Metal Face said casually and then turned and waved for the last gangbanger to move forward.

There was a gasp of surprise and fright from some of the customers when the fourth man came into the light. In his arms, in a neck lock, was Willy, and the teenager didn't look happy. His right arm was behind his back and he was good and stuck. It didn't help that the large man holding him was almost twice his size.

Metal Face held up his hands to calm everyone down.

"Now relax, people, just relax. We don't want no trouble. The kid is safe and he'll stay that way if Pops over here will just lower the gun and let us stay until whatever is happening outside has blown over."

"What about Willy? Are you gonna let him go?" Ted asked this, and I noticed his hands were clenched into fists. I looked to my right to see Bob moving closer to the gangbangers, as well, and I hoped he wasn't going to try something stupid.

"Yeah, man, abso-fucking-lutley. I had to grab him or else Grandpa would have shot me the instant I came over to the counter. All he is, is an insurance policy. Give me your word we're cool and I'll let him go, Grandpa. The kid's fine, Big Louie didn't hurt him."

"Is that true, Willy? You okay?" Norman asked while he held the shotgun. His hands were turning white as he squeezed the weapon in anger.

"Yeah, Grandpa, I'm fine. I heard them talking before they came up here. They just want to be in here with us, I don't think they want to hurt anyone."

Metal Face smiled. "See, what did I just say?"

Norman was biting his lip as he gave the problem some serious thinking. Fred moved closer to give his own advice.

"Norman, they have Willy and he's fine. When you think about it, you can't blame them for what they did. For all they knew, you would have shot them the moment you saw them in your store. I say let them stay. Besides, we might need their help before this is all over."

Norman's brow furrowed as he considered his options and finally he nodded. "Fine, we'll do it Fred's way. Okay, let Willy go and I promise you we won't try to go after you."

Metal Face smiled; the visage unsettling. "That's great, man, you made the right call, I promise." He turned to Big Louie. "Go 'head, bro, let the kid go."

Big Louie did what he was told and Willy stepped away from the large black man, rubbing his shoulder where it had been twisted behind him. He walked over to Norman and the rest of us, his face scrunched up in discomfort.

"You all right?" Ted asked.

"Yeah, I'm fine." He looked to Norman. "You want me to still get those flashlights and other stuff, Grandpa?"

Fred jumped in to answer. "Yes, please, Willy. As long as you're up to it. Nothing's changed; we still need them for light so we can see in here."

Willy glanced at Norman who nodded his consent, then Willy moved off again, passing by the four black men and giving them a wide berth. Metal face chuckled at this, but did nothing.

It was Ted who was the brave one, strolling over to the four black men with his hand held out in peace.

"So, you guys got names or what?" Ted asked with a smile. Metal Face didn't shake Ted's hand; instead he slapped Ted's hand and then rubbed the palm, followed by a tapping of the knuckles. I was middle-class white, but I knew that was the greeting some black men gave to one another, though I was clueless as to the proper way it should be done.

"I'm Grille, this is Slim and that's Quick. And the big guy is Big Louie."

"What's up," Big Louie said as he leaned against a display for Dutch Boy paint.

There were a few mumbled hellos, but everyone was still scared of these new people. Not that I blamed them one bit. These four black men looked like they would slit your throat for a dime and then kick you in the ass if all you had was a nickel. But I also knew sometimes people looked a certain way and in truth were harmless and were actually quite decent. Regardless of this, if I had been walking down the street and these four men had been coming my way, I would have immediately crossed the street to avoid them.

Metal Face glanced at Michelle and his lips spread wide. "And who is this little honey-pie?" He asked as he moved closer to her. She was still next to me, but was now standing. Though my heart was in my throat, I set Kyle down on the floor, and moved in between them. Kyle hugged my leg as he watched the adults talking. With a lump in my throat, I looked Metal Face--or Grille as I now knew his name-- straight in the eyes and placed my arm around Michelle.

"She's with me, and I'd appreciate it if you'd leave her alone."

Grille looked at me, sizing me up no doubt, and it was only when Bob moved next to me that Grille seemed to take a step back, raising his hands in an easy defensive manner with his palms facing me.

"Okay, man, she's with you, I got it, it's cool." He glanced at Bob. "Be cool, Hercules, no trouble here."

"Then why don't you go over there and stand for a while," Bob said, his arms crossed over his massive chest.

Grille nodded, and after a wink to Michelle, that said, I'll see you later; he walked back to his three friends.

"Thanks, Bob," I said to him as I breathed a sigh of relief.

"Anytime, John, anytime. I hate those assholes. Just give me an excuse."

"Well, you better keep your anger in check, Bob, because we got enough trouble around here without you starting a fight," Fred said as he stuck his finger in Bob's chest. Bob respected Fred and nodded like a scorned child. "Promise me, Bob, promise me you'll leave them alone," Fred ordered him.

"I promise," Bob said under his breath.

"Good, all right then, where were we before those men showed up?" Fred asked, wanting to get back to the problems at hand.

Fred's eyes glanced over each man and woman. Carl said nothing. He was like a mouse hiding from a cat. I didn't expect much more from him. Kyle wanted me to pick him up again, so I did, and he buried his head in my chest again.

He was scared and I didn't blame him one bit. I was just as scared, but I was trying to stay strong for my son. You never know just what you will do for your children until you're put in that situation. Sure, people talk a good game, saying they would sacrifice themselves in a second, but until you are truly thrust in a situation that could be your child's life or your own, that is when you know what you would or wouldn't do.

Anyone who says different is full of shit. No one knows what they will do until there is no time to think, but only do, fearless of the consequences.

A year ago, I took the family to Six Flags. They had this ride called the Screamer which was similar to the parachute drop. You were strapped into your seat and then the seat would shoot straight up about fifteen stories in less than three seconds. Once up there, the seats would stay in place and you were able to look straight down at the ground between your swinging feet. Despite the fact you are securely strapped in your chair, the feeling that your standing on a ledge is almost overwhelming. Well, in my ignorance of the ride, I brought Kyle with me. Once we were high in the air, Kyle began to panic, wanting to get out of his chair, even though to do that would be certain death. I should point out that I, too, was scared out of my mind, the feeling in my stomach was that sensation you get when you think you're going to die.

But because of Kyle panicking, the tears in his eyes welling up from his fear, I had no time to focus on my own distress. Instead, I talked my son down from panic, telling him to close his eyes and continually talking to him so he wouldn't freak out. What is it about a parent's voice that makes a child feel safe, even in a frightening situation such as this ride? Just by me staying calm and telling him he would be fine, he listened and after more than a minute, the ride dropped back to the earth and we were safe again. Needless to say, I will never go on that ride again. In dealing with my son's terror, I was able to block out my own, the love of my son overwhelming my own need for survival. I firmly believe I would have done anything to keep him in his seat, no matter how dangerous to myself.

And as I held his small body tightly against me, I knew I would do the same thing right now if needed in the moments to come.

After looking at Carl, Fred's eyes continued roving over the rest of us. When he was through, he counted us, his mouth moving as he did this. "Hey, we're one short," he said. "Who's missing?"

I joined Fred in searching the faces, trying to remember each person, and in a second I figured it out. It was George Lipton. He was nowhere to be seen.

"It's George, he's not here," I said out loud.

Voices answered me. "Hey, that's right, he's gone," one voice said. "Where'd he go?" Another added. "Maybe he's in the bathroom," another one said, one of the gay guys I think.

All faces turned at the sounds of footsteps running towards us from one of the dark aisles. Norman had a small penlight, similar to the one he had given Willy, and he flashed it down the center aisle. It was Willy and he was running at us like a sprinter.

"What's wrong, son, where's the fire?" Fred asked as he moved to the teenager. Willy pointed to the back room, where Norman kept all his overstock. "There's some guy back there. He's trying to get the loading dock door open. He was saying something about wanting to get home to his family."

"What? That door is locked, he can't get it open without a key. I had some thefts a few months ago so I make sure the doors locked on the inside at all times," Norman said as he held up a set of keys.

Ted moved closer to Norman. "What about the fire door, you got one of those?"

Norman's face went wide with surprise. "Shit, yes I do. And all he has to do is press down on the bar and it opens automatically, though it sticks a lot in the summer and you kind of have to push it at an odd angle to the right. I haven't locked it yet. I only do that at the end of the day."

"Then we still have time to stop him," Bob said and took off at a run. Everyone knew where the back room was that lived in Revere and shopped at Sterns. Not only did the large room hold overstock of supplies, but that was where Norman kept his beer and snacks for those late night poker games. The table used for re-screening doors and windows would be cleaned off and Norman would toss a table cloth onto it. Then he and his pals would play long into the night. Of course, all this was a few years ago, back when his wife was still alive and he needed to hide from her after she'd left the hardware store for the day.

I handed Kyle to Michelle and she took him like it was the most natural thing in the world. Kyle didn't argue, and seemed to take to Michelle, as well. I think it was just that he missed his mother and Michelle was female. Any port in the storm, as the saying goes. With Ted, Norman, and one of the older men who I didn't know, we all followed Bob to the back room.

I rounded the corner and was entering the back room just as Bob reached the fire door and George.

George had figured out how to open it and was already stepping through the open doorway, and Bob reached out and grasped George's right arm in a vise-like grip.

Not knowing it at the time, I noticed an acrid smell in the air, coming from the open door. It reminded me of sulfur, but with a sweet fragrance mixed in. I wrinkled my nose and ignored it.

"Now, just wait a second there, pal, I thought we were gonna discuss this," Bob said in a gasping voice as he tried to pull the smaller man inside.

"Leave me alone, please, my family needs me!" George yelled while trying to free himself from Bob's strong hands. Bob had managed to pull George halfway back inside the back room and was about to give him a final yank to complete the job. I looked beyond George and out into what should have been the back lot of the hardware store, but instead there was nothing but blackness. A deep, inky obsidian that absorbed the small amount of light cast off from the two backup lights on the back room's walls, just a few inches from the ceiling.

But then I saw a shape morph out of the blackness. It was a pale-gray with no eyes and had the shape of a scorpion and a millipede if they had successfully mated, but without the stinger. There were two large pincers in front of its mouth, similar to what you would find on an ant, each three times the size of a grown man's hand. The red orifice I assumed was its mouth was round and puckered and contained twin rows of hooked teeth, much like a tapeworm.

But any resemblance to a creature from earth ended there. One difference was this creature was the size of a large dog and the second was its speed. I blinked twice, wondering if I was seeing things, but then I remembered what had jumped at the glass doors earlier and had tried to enter the hardware store, but Bob had locked the doors in time.

"George, behind you!" I screamed to the man, hoping my warning was in time as I pointed to the nightmarish thing behind him.

George never saw what attacked him. One second he was fighting Bob to get free, the next, the creature had jumped onto his back and began ripping at his flesh. Blood splashed into the air as the creature slashed with its pincers, George's shrieks of pain filling the back room.

Bob let go of George then, falling away, and a scream left George's lips as he turned his head and stared at something fabricated from his nightmares. Behind me, others yelled and called out, and one voice prayed for God to save them.

As for George, he had changed his tune and was now fighting desperately to toss the creature off him and get back inside the safety of the back room, shrieking at the top of his lungs for us to help him while the creature ripped into him.

I was the first to break from the shock of seeing something impossible and I dashed forward to help George. When I moved, the others did, as well, and as a team we charged at George, each of us grabbing an arm as we desperately tried to get him back inside the room and close the door.

But he was stuck, and try as we might, his body wouldn't break free of whatever was holding him. He actually slipped back a foot, but Bob placed his right leg on the doorframe, bracing himself like an anchor, and with another heave, we all yanked backwards again.

George's blood splashed onto the floor like scarlet rain, painting the floor the color of death.

7

GEORGE SPLITS UP

TERRORS IN THE DARK

CASUALTIES

IN MY ENTIRE lifetime, I had seen another human being seriously hurt just once. I mean to the point that blood actually gushed out of the wound.

I was nine or ten, I'm not sure exactly, but I know it was the second winter after the rat incident. I lived on a dead end, the railroad tracks at the end of the street. If you crossed the tracks, the road would continue and sometimes some really crazy drivers would drive over the tracks, their suspensions bouncing like they were driving on the moon. After that had happened more than once, the city put up jersey barriers and a few metal poles to stop automobiles from trying to cross the tracks.

It was the middle of winter when the incident I remember happened. We had a lot of snow that year and the plows would push a lot of the ice and snow from the main road into my dead end and the one across the tracks from me. The hills of dirty ice were perfect for sledding and me and more than a dozen of my friends would have a ball. Sometimes though, we would have to stop while the train drove down the tracks. The tracks are dead now; no longer in use, and I see them sometimes when I cut through Malden on an errand. Now they are dirty and rusty with weeds growing over them as Mother Nature tries to reclaim what was once hers. I have fond memories of playing with the train on those tracks; all except one, of course.

Sometimes in the summer, my friends and I would place coins or rocks on the tracks and wait until the train's massive metal wheels would drive over the items. The coins were always squished flat and would be rendered worthless, but it was just so neat to see the incredible weight of the train compact the metal. A few times we even turned into juvenile delinquents and put a shopping carriage or an old couch on the tracks. The train would never slow, but would just plow over the couch or cart, knocking them aside like they were nothing more than bales of straw. Often, after one such incident, my friends and I would discuss what could happen to a person stupid enough to get in the way of the train.

So, on one snowy winter's day, we all played on the icy hills, sliding down them and then climbing back up to do it again. Back then, in the seventies, parents gave their children much more freedom then nowadays and there were no parents in sight watching us. We were totally alone. The oldest of us was probably eleven, the youngest maybe seven.

We had to stop sledding when the sounds of the train began. The train would blast its horn, warning of its approach and you could feel the tracks actually vibrate, as if they were a living thing all on their own. In the summer, you could place your ear to the tracks and actually feel the train coming long before you ever saw it.

So with the horn blaring, all of us climbed to the top of the tallest hill and sat on our sleds, waiting for the train to pass so we could continue sledding. But there was this one boy, Brandon Nelson, who was sitting closest to the edge of the hill. As the train approached, he shifted on his sled, and before any of us realized it, he had lost his balance and was sliding down the hill directly towards the tracks.

Yells of panic filled the air and a few of us charged down the slope to catch him, but he was going far too fast to stop. The train continued on, the horn sounding the only warning. Even if the engineer had wanted to, it was very unlikely he could have stopped in time.

Brandon had his hands out, as he tried to stop his fateful slide, but gravity would not be denied and he slid all the way to the tracks. It was almost like God had timed it to happen, the way events had lined up so perfectly.

Brandon was spread out flat on the tracks, his entire body covering both steel rods when two of my friends reached him. The train was now only a few feet away and the tension in the air was so thick it could be tasted.

They grabbed a leg each and the two boys began dragging Brandon off the tracks, but they were just a little too slow, and just before Brandon was completely off the tracks, the train reached him. Only Brandon's left hand was still on the track and the train ran over his fingers, slicing them like a hot knife through butter.

I'll never forget the shriek of pain Brandon sent into the frigid air and the gasp from all of us watching. Brandon was dragged free of the tracks and the train continued on, perhaps never knowing what had transpired. When the train had rolled past, one of the boys ran to the tracks and picked up two of Brandon's fingers, holding them in the air as if they were a prize. The other two fingers on Brandon's hand were still attached, though only by the inside flap of skin. Blood shot into the air to stain the snow red and I still remember the copper taste that filled my nose and mouth as the air filled with the fragrance of fresh-spilled blood.

With all the screaming, one of the nearby homes heard the commotion and an adult came running. After that, Brandon was brought to the hospital where I found out later they managed to reattach all his fingers. A happy ending in the end, but something that never left me. After that, no parent would let their child go near those tracks and for good reason.

So when I saw George Lipton holding onto the doorframe and blood dripping onto the floor, I was truly shocked. I'd seen countless movies where the victim is chopped and cut up into little, bitty pieces, but to see it really happening, to smell the bile and taste the blood in your mouth, well, that is an entirely different ballgame.

I was so pumped on adrenalin, I was still able to react and I grabbed George by the left arm as Bob and Ted grabbed his other. Both of us held on tight, and then as one, began pulling him back inside the door. While we pulled, the creature on his back scurried lower on his body and disappeared into the darkness.

"Come on, pull!" Bob yelled as he yanked as hard as he could. But as I said, it was as if something was holding George back.

George's voice was growing hoarse as he screamed again and again. His head was shaking back and forth as if he still couldn't believe what was happening to him, and his hair flopped around like a living thing all its own. The veins in his forehead pulsed and I swear I could see them beating in synch with his heart.

Then the creature climbed onto George's back again and perched like a bird on his shoulders. It hissed at us and we all jumped away, George's precarious grip holding onto the doorframe the only thing keeping him from being pulled into the unknown darkness. His hands were bone-white, a death-grip, I think they call it, and he continued to shake his head no.

None of us knew what to do; we sure didn't want to get close to that nightmare and risk getting attacked ourselves. It was the old man who solved the problem. Finding a brand new pitchfork from somewhere in the back room, he charged at the creature and jabbed it right between the pincers. There was a high-pitched squeal that would have made a dog deaf and it skittered back down George's back, taking the pitchfork with it when the handle was ripped from his hands.

Bob was the first to go into action, jumping back to grab George's hand with Ted and I both following. Something told me this was our last chance to save George. It had to be because, whether it was my imagination or not, I could have sworn I saw other shapes in the darkness, just waiting to enter the hardware store.

"Okay, guys, on three!" Bob yelled. And then counted. "One, two…Three!"

All three of us yanked as hard as we could and George flew into the room to strike the floor hard. I fell backward, and struck my head on the concrete floor; I was dizzy for a second and I saw the world spin. I could hear more screaming, and at first assumed it was George, but as I sat up and my eyes focused, I saw it was Bob screaming, as well as Ted. At first I didn't understand what was wrong. What could make, big, macho Bob scream like a girl? And then my eyes followed where they were looking and my mouth fell open and I felt my own scream growing in my chest.

There was George, now safe inside the room, but there wasn't as much of him as when I had seen him last. From the waist down there was nothing left of him, his legs were gone. Intestines slid out of him like pink snakes, and bile and stomach juice slopped across the floor. A whiff came to my nose and I could already feel the heaves, my stomach wanting to expel breakfast.

I think the worst thing of all was that George was still alive, and he weakly flailed with his hands, reaching for one of us to help him. Though I'm not proud of myself, I cracked and began crawling backwards, just wanting to get away from the monstrosity that was once a man. George looked me straight in the eyes and I saw the light go out. It is truly hard to describe what it really looks like to see that light disappear, but I would have to say it was like, just before George died, he seemed to be looking over me, or through me, instead of at me. Then his eyes seemed to shift away to look somewhere else altogether and his head dropped to the floor.

For what seemed like an hour, but was probably only five or ten seconds, no one spoke or uttered a single sound. We all stared at the mutilated body of George with utter shock filling us with dread.

Then, out of the darkness the creature appeared. But it didn't care about us, at least not now. Its pincers were stained a dull red from where it had been burrowing into George's back and it hissed at us again. Before any of us could do anything, it shot forward the few feet to George, and its pincers latched onto a particularly juicy pair of intestines, and then, like a leash, it backed out of the room and through the doorway, dragging George's half-corpse with it like a child's toy on a string.

No one did a thing, happy to let the creature take its prize. But no sooner did it leave, then two more took its place. They clicked their pincers and moved forward a foot, their multiple legs clicking on the stone floor.

"Close that damn door before more get in here!" The old man yelled, breaking us from our fugue state. Bob was the first up and he looked around for a weapon. He found it in a metal rake hanging with a few other yard supplies. Ripping the rake from the wall, he poked at the far left creature like he was using a spear. The other one jumped away and scuttled into the back room, its legs clicking like a hundred tap dancers running. When it moved from the door, Bob reached out and grabbed the door handle, pulling it shut with a clang. At least no more could get in, but then how were we supposed to get rid of these two?

I rolled away and Ted helped me up, both of us staring at the creature. The old man tossed us each a broomstick, used for replacements when the wooden shaft would break on a tool. With the sticks in hand, we both began to try and whack the creature before it tried to get by us and into the hardware store. If it got by us, we would never be able to stop it, the hardware store being quite large. Then I thought of Kyle, and I vowed this abomination would not get past me.

Bob was handling his own creature, and he whacked it again and again. But the shell of the creature was able to withstand the blows, much like a beetle or cockroach. But at least he was able to halt it until it managed to crawl away from him and scuttle onto the wall. Its feet had suction and it moved back and forth while Bob picked at it again and again. Finally, he scored a good shot and the creature fell back to the floor, landing on its back, but immediately spun back onto its legs.

As for me and Ted, we continued to push our monster backward, keeping it from getting around us. But with only a rake and sticks, there was no useful way to kill these things. It didn't help that both creatures were as big as a full-grown German Shepherd.

"Hey, you, old man, come here and take this rake from me," Bob yelled. The old man did as he was told, and when he got to Bob, he smiled. "Name's Peter, son, not old man."

Bob nodded, his eyes never leaving the multi-legged creature. "Fair enough, Peter, here, take this and try to keep this fucker from moving. I've got an idea how to stop this shit once and for all."

Peter did as he was told, taking the rake and poking the thing. A few times the pincers grabbed the end of the rake, but it was made of metal and the prongs didn't cut, though the rake did bend from the pressure and shiny marks appeared, scraped into the paint. It was easy to see how George had been cut in half like a pork roast.

"I'll be right back, hold tight," Bob said and ran by us, back into the hardware store.

That was all we could do, poking and prodding as the two creatures tried to attack us. We continued for almost five minutes and I was starting to get worried when Bob came back, pushing a shopping cart. In the shadows of the back room, I had no idea what he'd brought back with him, but it was a couple of bags of some kind. He picked one up and threw it across his chest and then hopped up onto the table used for screening doors and windows. The table legs groaned from the weight and I wondered if it would hold.

"Here, get one of them bastards over here! Get it under me!" Bob yelled.

"We'll do it," I told Peter as we were closest to the table. Peter grunted in agreement, but he was much too busy trying to keep the giant creature at bay for conversation. A few times it tried to jump over him and he barely managed to get out of the way. He was old, at least eighty, and his muscles didn't work as well as they once did. In one flash of light I saw his face was beaded in sweat and he looked like he was laboring for breath.

Ted and I began trying to push our monster towards Bob. He was standing on the table now, looking down on us all and I still had no idea what he was up to.

It was me that finally got the thing where Bob needed it. When I poked it hard in the mouth, it grabbed my stick and tried to eat it. The stick slid almost a foot into its red gash of a mouth and the instant it did, I used my arms to shift my weight and slid it across the floor. It was heavy and my muscles strained with effort, but I did it.

"Hurry, I don't know how long I can hold it!" I told Bob, but I needn't have bothered. In the dull shadows of the emergency lights, Bob lifted the bag higher over his head and then lined up the giant creature. Then he dropped what he was holding right on top of the back of the creature. The fifty pound bag of cement slammed the body to the floor and the carapace cracked like a boiled egg being crushed by a slapping hand. A noxious yellow fluid splattered across the floor and one wall and Ted was the first to see the liquid hissing.

"Holy, shit," Ted exclaimed, "it's like in that Alien Movie, the goddamn blood is like acid. Look at that shit burn!"

I looked where Ted was pointing, and in the shadows, I watched the floor as it hissed with the burning blood. Then it stopped. Where the blood was there were now pits in the concrete and I didn't have to wonder what that blood would do to human skin.

"Uh, guys, I need some help here!" Peter gasped as the rake was ripped from his hands and the scorpion-like thing lunged for him. We tried to stop it, but it was too late and the creature managed to get its pincers around Peter's left leg, and like a guillotine, snipped his foot off just above the ankle like a florist trimming a rose.

Peter screamed to the heavens and blood shot out of his leg like a hose with each beat of his heart. The scorpion was bathed in scarlet and it seemed to jump for joy as it tried to lick up the sticky fluid, its puckered mouth moving in and out.

"Jesus Christ!" I yelled as I pulled my broomstick out of the dead thing a few feet away and charged at the one attacking Peter. When I got close enough, I watched Peter's foot disappear into its gaping maw and it reminded me a little of a lobster's mouth. I realize now that I was trying desperately to take this nightmarish creature and in some way make it identify with a creature I knew existed.

My blood ran cold as I imagined myself being devoured by this creature that seemed to look on human beings as lunch. Ted moved next to me a second later and we both began whacking at it with our broomsticks.

Then Bob came from behind us and he had another bag of cement in his hands. It was high over his head and his arms flexed with the weight. I honestly don't think I could have done such a feat. Bob pushed past us, dodged out of the way of the pincers and brought the cement bag down hard, using his own strength to help gravity. The bag landed on the head of the creature and the back end was raised into the air, like if a car was crushed only on the front bumper and the back would jump into the air before coming back to earth.

There was another high-pitched squeal and the creature's legs went crazy. It shuddered for almost a minute and finally remained still. More yellow ichor seeped out and steamed onto the floor, etching its flow pattern into the stone.

Peter cried out in pain and we all turned to him. Bob grabbed a stack of rags and ripped one in two, wrapping it around his leg above the wound where Peter's foot had been and trying to stop the blood. I stared at them both, not knowing what to do. A small part of my mind, the rational side still alive, told me that Peter was as good as dead. Without a doctor, how would we seal his ghastly wound? The answer was we couldn't.

Fire might work, we could cauterize it, but I didn't think I could do that even if asked. I suggested it to Ted and he nodded; running back into the hardware store to get some lighter fluid to make a torch.

Peter was spread out on the floor now, his breathing coming in gasps. His complexion was pale, and when I leaned down and touched his hand, and took it in my own, I felt his skin; it was ice cold. He turned his head and stared up at me and I was shocked when he smiled slightly.

"It's okay, son. I'm an old man and probably didn't have much time left on this earth anyway."

"Don't say that. That's crazy. You have another decade at least." I looked to Bob, who shook his head sadly. There was a large pool of Peter's blood covering the floor, a lot of it mixing with George's blood, but it was still obvious if Peter didn't get to a hospital very, very, soon he would probably die. Not to mention there seemed to be a growing infection already spreading on his leg, just above where the foot was severed. Blue and black lines were already rising up his leg to disappear under his pant leg. Whatever those things were made of, they were toxic to humans.

And Peter seemed to know this.

He winced in pain and squeezed my hand tight. It hurt, he squeezed so tightly, but I said nothing, merely gazed down at this man who I had just fought beside and didn't even know his last name.

Ted charged back into the room, making sure to give the crushed carapace by the table a wide berth. I looked up at him to see he had brought the supplies to make a torch, but Peter's grip had already lessened, and when I turned away from Ted to gaze back down on Peter's face, I could see his eyes were not moving and his mouth was slightly agape. I touched his throat, feeling around for a pulse like I'd seen on television, but after a full thirty seconds I was pretty sure he was gone.

I closed his eyes and laid his hands on top of one another on his chest, then I looked to Bob and Ted.

"He's gone," I said softly.

"Shit, that sucks. I liked this old guy, he was a tough one," Bob said.

I had nothing to say in reply so I said nothing.

Suddenly, the silence was broken when a large thump filled the room. All eyes turned to the fire door and we all jumped an inch when it thumped again, a small dent appearing in the smooth surface.

"Jesus Christ, there's more of them out there and they want in badly," I said in horror.

"Think that door'll hold?" Ted asked.

Bob answered by standing and shrugging. "Don't know, but maybe we should fill some of the others in on what's happening and see if Norman has any ideas on how to reinforce that door."

There was an old tarp in the corner and I went to it, picked it up and opened it over Peter, then laid it over his body. It would have to do for now as there was nowhere else to put him.

Another thing struck the door, only this one wasn't as intense.

"Maybe they'll get bored when they can't get in," Ted suggested as he looked at me and Bob.

Neither of us answered him; there was really nothing to say.

"Come on, let's get back to the others," Bob said and began moving back into the main store. He paused when he reached the dead creature by the table. "If we're gonna stay here, we're probably gonna have to figure out what to do with these things, too."

"One thing at a time, huh?" I asked while I followed him out of the back room. Another thud filled the room behind me, but thankfully, the intensity was less this time. Maybe Ted was right and the creatures would just give up when they couldn't get in. No one seemed to want to tackle the problem of just where in the hell they had come from yet.

It was as we were walking through the store, and the counter was right in front of us, that another problem surfaced in my head that chilled me to the bone.

It was what was behind the counter actually.

Behind the counter was the front wall of the hardware store. A front wall made of nothing but plate-glass and metal framing. Not to mention the double-glass doors. They were made of heavy duty glass, as well, but the question was, were they strong enough to deflect an attack from those creatures?

I moved to Kyle and Michelle handed him to me with a smile. I squeezed him so tight he told me to take it easy. Walking to the double doors, I gazed out into the darkness, wondering what was waiting for us in those inky depths.

With no answer, I hugged Kyle tighter.

8

CATCHING UP

DISAGREEMENTS

WHILE I STARED out the double doors of the store, Bob and Ted went straight for Fred and Norman, taking the two men aside to begin telling the tale of what had happened to George and Peter.

I didn't get involved. I felt I had done enough for the moment and was only going to worry about Kyle for a while. Besides, Ted and Bob didn't need me to tell Fred and Norman what had happened.

I watched Bob lead Norman and Fred to the back of the store, assuming they were going to be shown the two dead creatures. They were gone for a good fifteen minutes, and when they returned, both Fred and Norman wore washed out looks of shock. Fred came straight for me, his eyes wide with disbelief, but believing just the same. "You all right, John?"

"Yeah, Fred, as all right as any of us can be in a time like this." I was thinking about Karen again. If those things were everywhere, then what was happening at the house? The windows would never stop those creatures. Would she hide in the attic or the basement? Would she even have time before one or more of them tried to attack her? I didn't know and the not knowing was driving me crazy.

"Yeah, I know what you mean. We got some serious problems to deal with and I hope you'll be a part of the solution."

"Yeah, Fred, I'm there, just let me know, but right now I just want to be alone with my son."

He nodded, patted my shoulder and walked away to join the others at the counter. He paused as he turned away from me. "I sure hope Margie's okay."

Before I could answer, he left, leaving me to stare out the doors again into the darkness.

It was lighter in front of the hardware store now, Willy having found all the oil lanterns, flashlights and batteries, plus a few candles scattered here and there. There were four groups of people at the moment, all gathered in different parts of the store. There were the gangbangers in the back of the store, who were their own island unto themselves, there was Norman and his little group, and there was Judith with the young married couple and the two gay men. I watched the two men for a few minutes when they weren't looking at me and I definitely saw some hand action. Yeah, they were gay. That was fine with me, more power to 'em.

"I miss Mommy," Kyle said out of nowhere. He had been relatively quiet since the dark had fallen and I was glad he was talking again, though not the question he chose to use as his first words in a while.

"Yeah, champ, I miss her, too," I told him.

"Do you think we can go see her soon?" He asked this with such a casual tone, like it was no big deal. Kyle didn't know anything about the creatures or what had happened in the back room.

I nodded slightly. "Sure, champ, soon, we just need to stay here a little while longer."

He cocked his head to the side as if he was giving it some thought. "Daddy, where did the sun go?"

That was a damn good question and God how I wish I had an answer for him.

"I don't know, buddy, I really don't."

"Will it come back soon?"

"I don't know, Kyle; there are some things daddies just don't know. All we can do is wait and see what happens next. You can be brave for me, right?"

He nodded, pushing his chest out as I held him. "Sure can."

"That's good, that's real good." I looked over my shoulder to see Michelle standing alone near the plumbing section. Her face was creased with worry as she looked around at the faces she didn't know. Her arms were wrapped around herself protectively and I decided I'd had enough alone time with Kyle, so I left the glass doors and joined Michelle.

"Hey," I said, almost shyly.

"Hey, yourself. I heard some of the guys talking and is it true what they're saying?" Her blue eyes reflected the candle light nearby and I thought how beautiful she looked. Then a guilty feeling flooded through me and I tried to push the growing feelings I guess I still had for this woman back down. I loved my wife, and I had to remember that. She could be fighting for her life right now and I'm thinking about how nice it would be to get into Michelle's pants. What was wrong with me?

"You mean about the things in the dark?" I asked.

"Uh-huh, yes, is it really true?"

"I'm afraid so, but we should be safe in here." I decided not to say anything about the plate-glass windows. What was there to say? There wasn't enough wood in the store to cover them even if we wanted to, so what was the point?

"I hope so. God, this is so crazy, like something out of a Stephen King book."

"Oh yeah, you like Stephen King?" I asked her. Karen didn't read for pleasure and often chastised me for reading horror novels, saying they were a waste of time.

"You bet, I read everything he writes. The last one I read was about the guy on the lake who can paint pictures that come true."

I shook my head. "Haven't gotten that one yet, was it good?"

"Yeah, I liked it, a little long, but you know how he is." She shifted position and my eyes dropped to her chest. I couldn't help but admire the way the material brushed against her bra, conforming to every curve. I found myself getting a very unwanted erection and put Kyle down, covering my waist with my shirt. I felt like a high school boy who had gotten a woody just before I had to go to the blackboard to write down a problem.

I nodded, agreeing with her about her opinion on King. That was exactly how he was, but I liked it that way. You got to know the characters as people before the shit would hit the fan. I found myself warming up to Michelle even more. It was nice to be able to talk to someone about something I enjoyed so much.

We sat down together with Kyle in between us and chatted some more about some other things that interested us both. I found we had a lot in common and was remembering why I had dated her in the first place.

"So, why did you come back to Boston? I thought you were going to leave?" I asked her.

"Yes, and I did, but you know how it is. After a while you get homesick and my family is here." Her face grew serious and I figured she was thinking about her family and friends, but then she brushed it off. "Plus, all the jobs are in the Boston area, there wasn't much in my field where I was."

"Oh, and what field is that?"

"Business management," she replied and shifted position on the floor. Once again my eyes dropped and I couldn't help but follow the curve of her thigh to where it met in the middle. Her jeans were tight and showed off her great legs. I shifted position myself, pulling my shirt down more. Next to me, Kyle was playing with his wrestler. I hadn't even known he still had it with him and guessed he must have hidden it in one of his pockets.

"Daddy, I'm bored," he said, setting the action figure down.

"Hang in there for a little while longer and I'll see if I can scrounge you up something to play with, okay?"

He nodded and went back to playing. He was being so good, and I could only pray he would hang in there a little longer.

Glancing over my shoulder, the men were standing around the counter. Norman, Ted, Fred, Bob and the other older man I didn't know were all talking quietly. Carl was there, too, but he was standing near the perimeter, by Ted. He was saying nothing and barely listening. I had a feeling he was in shock, not that I could blame him. Buddy and Earl were standing slightly to the side, talking alone.

One of the gay men stood up and walked over to me and Michelle. He smiled as he squatted down on his haunches. I noticed his khaki pants, the Hush Puppies on his feet and a polo shirt that could have come right out of an Abercrombie catalog.

"Hey, my name's Jordan, and I hope you don't mind, but I made this for your son."

In his hand was a small toy car, with carved wheels and a racing stripe. It had been made from a small block of wood and when I looked over to where he was I saw a small pile of woodchips.

"Did you just carve this?" I asked him.

"Yeah, it's a hobby of mine. Keeps me busy and I needed something to take my mind off of what's happening. My partner and me took the train in from Cambridge and look what happens? Now we're alone in a city we don't know and there's something unbelievable happening."

"Well, I'm John, this is Kyle, and this pretty lady is Michelle," I said, holding out my hand for him to take. "Thank you, this is really kind of you," I told him as I shook his hand. "Say, you want to sit down and talk with us for a while?"

Jordan shook his head. "Nah, I'm good, maybe later if the offer's still there. Shaun needs me right now. He's kind of the worrying type and you can imagine how he feels right now."

"Sure," I said, "the offer is always open. Whenever you want to, come on over."

"I'll do that. And nice meeting you, all of you. You enjoy that car, okay?" Jordan said to Kyle. Kyle nodded yes. He was already playing with it and that was as good as an endorsement Jordan was going to get that he liked it. Michelle said thank you as well and bid Jordan goodbye.

I checked my watch and saw it was almost two o' clock in the afternoon. I had set out to go to the market late in the morning and hours had past like a time warp. With the sun gone and no light outside the store, it was hard to gauge time. I wondered how I would feel come nightfall, not that there would be one. It was always night now and once again I wondered if whatever was happening would end or if this was how it was going to be forever. And if it was, what was the fate of us and the earth itself? Without light, the trees would die, oxygen wouldn't be made and I guess all life on earth would cease to exist. So even if we managed to survive, sooner or later we would starve or die of oxygen deficiency or perhaps even an ice age. Then again, maybe this was some kind of massive solar eclipse and in time it would simply pass. So many unknowns and no answers.

As I daydreamed and thought about things that were far beyond my control, I didn't notice that Grille had joined Fred and the others at the counter. I only noticed him when his voice rose an octave or two and then he began to yell at Norman. Fred tried to calm Grille down, but the man would have none of it.

"This is bullshit, all of it. You white people are crazy. Monsters in the dark, that's ridiculous. This is nothing more than another eclipse or some shit. It'll be over soon and then me and my crew will leave this looney bin."

"But then how do you explain the things in the back room, huh?" Fred asked, trying to sound rational. "What about the body and all the blood?"

Grille waved his hand in a dismissive gesture at Fred and the others.

"I don't give a shit, man; it's probably some Halloween decorations that you did up with some goop to make us think you're telling the truth. And the old dude probably died of a heart attack and the other guy simply left through the back door. You just want us to leave, that's all."

"If we wanted you to leave, we wouldn't have let you stay in the first place," Ted said, trying to reason with Grille.

"It didn't hurt that they took my grandson hostage," Norman said. "Black pieces of shit," he mumbled the last part under his breath, but I still heard it. I was just glad Grille hadn't. If he had, I think things might have went real bad, real fast

"Fine, then if you think we're telling lies, then why don't you just leave right now?" Bob asked, offended that he was being called a liar. "If I'm lying about what I saw and fought back there, then why don't you just go now? Why are you even staying in here with us?"

Grille opened his mouth to answer, but nothing came out. I knew the answer for Grille, even if the man didn't. It was because he was scared. He was as frightened as the rest of us, but his male pride wouldn't let him admit it to himself or his friends.

Instead, he waved us away and began walking back to his three friends.

"Forget it, you guys, crazy-ass white, motherfuckers, you're all whacked in the head."

"No, wait, come on, we need to talk about this, we need to stick together here," Fred said, but Grille wasn't listening.

He spun one last time and made eye contact with each man who returned his gaze. "Tell you what, you guys stay over there and me and my boys will stay back here. When this shit ends, we're gone; end of story." Then he spun and walked down the aisle to be swallowed by the darkness in the store.

I was close enough to hear Fred talking to the other men and I listened closely.

"This isn't good, you know, we all need to stick together here."

"Fuck 'em. Let them stay back there and rot for all I care. Didn't want them in my store to begin with," Norman said angrily. His racism was so apparent he should have just put on a pointed white hood and sheet and start dancing around a burning cross.

"Don't say that, Grandpa. If what Bob and Ted said is true, and I believe 'em, then we're gonna need everyone to stay safe, and I don't think those things outside care if your black or white." Willy said this and I thought how ironic that the grandson was wiser then the grandfather.

Norman made a dismissive sound in his throat and turned away from the counter, crossing his arms. For good or bad, he was finished talking for the moment.

After that encounter with Grille, everything seemed to quiet down. The three groups stayed together, talking amongst themselves and I guess you could say Michelle, Kyle and I made up the fourth group. With it being so dark in the store and no sun outside, it didn't take long for Kyle to get sleepy. I found a couple bags of mechanic rags in one of the aisles and opened them, then spread them out so Kyle had something soft to sleep on. For a blanket, not that we needed one as it was warm in the store, I covered him with a beach towel from the seasonal section. Being near the beach, Norman always had a summer section filled with handy items people might need on the go. It was still summer and warm in the store, but with each passing hour the temperature dropped slightly and I wondered how cold it might get.

With Kyle sleeping, Michelle and I continued to talk and I found myself falling for her hard all over again. Yes, I still loved my wife, but she wasn't with me and I was scared, not knowing what the future might bring. After witnessing two people dying in the space of half a day, I was also aware of my own mortality more than ever. If I was going to die, would it really be so bad to seek the comfort of the person who was with me? It felt good to make a connection with someone else, as selfish as that might sound. As for Kyle, I tried not to think about what would happen to him if one of those creatures got to him. Thinking about him being killed and eaten by those things outside made it too hard to even function. I had to push those thoughts out of my head or risk going insane.

The hours went by and everyone relaxed, if only slightly. A few dozed off and others merely closed their eyes and tried to sleep, even though it wouldn't come. Grille's gang was nowhere to be found. They had set up in the far back of the store and no one bothered them. Norman, Fred, Ted and a few others were playing poker by oil lantern, using nuts, bolts and washers as currency. Different items were worth different dollar amounts, like poker chips.

After more hours had gone by, I checked my watch to see it was going on seven-thirty. My stomach rumbled and I knew when Kyle woke up, he too, would be hungry. All of us were. It had been almost half a day we'd been trapped inside the hardware store and we would all need to eat soon.

I decided when Kyle woke I would talk to Fred and Norman about food. There was a candy rack near the counter, filled with chips and candy bars and cases of soda stacked near the door for tourists going to the beach. No one would go hungry, at least not yet.

I glanced at Michelle to see her eyes were closed. Her chest rose and fell in rhythm with her breathing and I watched her sleep for a full five minutes. Unhindered about discovery, my eyes roamed over her body. I studied the smooth skin of her neck, her perfectly formed lips, her manicured eyebrows, and the slight cleavage line from her bra. If I looked hard enough, I thought I could just see the outline of one of her nipples through the fabric of her shirt. I gazed at the small hairs on the back of her arms and noticed the light fuzz on her cheeks, only seen if the dull light was at just the right angle.

I still felt guilty about how I felt, but I also knew I couldn't deny these feelings. I wanted her, more than any other woman except for Karen. And I desperately wished I could hold my wife in my arms at least one more time. But I couldn't. She was miles away and I didn't even know if she was still alive.

But Michelle was still alive and was sitting right next to me and I wanted her.

If that was wrong, then I was wrong. She stirred in her sleep and I immediately looked away, embarrassed for staring at her. The mood was broken and I felt a wash of exhaustion fill me. Touching Kyle's head softly, and making sure he was all right, I leaned back and closed my eyes, trying to get some rest, as well.

With my eyes closed, I never noticed when the backup lights scattered about the store died, the batteries they were connected to finally drained of power.

9

INFILTRATION

THEY CAME IN the middle of the night, though with it always dark, I only assumed it was night, as there was no time to check my watch.

Unknown to any of us at the time, there was an air vent situated at the top right of the plate-glass windows in the front of the store. The vent had a fan inside it and Norman would use this when it wasn't that hot or cold outside, and by doing this, he could ventilate the store without running his heating or air conditioning. If you add the ceiling fans scattered across the ceiling, he was able to keep the climate inside the hardware store comfortable for his customers.

The vent was open at the moment and more than two dozen cat-sized scorpion creatures entered the hardware store. They were silent, their small legs adhering to the wall and ceiling like spiders and it was only luck that they were spotted before they did more damage to our small group of refugees.

Of all the people to sound the alarm, it was Carl who saved the day. Later that night, when things had calmed down, he filled me in on what had happened and how he came to be the hero of our little group.

He told me how he had a weak bladder and had woken from a light sleep to use the bathroom at the rear of the store. So far the water still worked, perhaps because the pipes were underground, but all of us had partaken of the porcelain bowl at least one time since entering the store.

When he had stood up and scratched his face with exhaustion, he looked up at the ceiling to see a dozen shadows crisscrossing the ceiling in between the hanging, now defunct, florescent light fixtures, thanks to the two flickering candles left on while everyone slept. He had a flashlight in his hand, but didn't want to turn it on, not wanting to bother any of the sleeping people scattered around him on the floor, but when he saw those shadows moving above him, he flicked it on, aiming the tight beam at the ceiling.

That was when he screamed, waking everyone in the store, and I snapped awake with fear in my throat and my hand reaching out for Kyle. There were multiple yells and questions asked as everyone tried to figure out what was happening. Looking back now, we should have kept someone on watch at all times, but we were new to this idea of being under siege and we had thought we were safe inside the building.

The first real screams began a second after Carl sounded the alarm. Like a starter pistol had been fired at the start of a race, all the creatures dropped from the ceiling at the same time to land on the floor around us, pincers snapping at exposed flesh.

I noticed that sweet and acrid smell of sulfur again and later would realize it must have been the creatures.

"Michelle, take Kyle and protect him for me," I told her while I handed her my son. She didn't argue, but hugged him tightly, moving away from any shadows nearby. Kyle was crying; scared, but not knowing why because he couldn't see what was happening yet.

It was almost pitch-black in the store and one of the candles had blown out, leaving visibility to nothing. But then, like the morning sunrise, Norman and his grandson lit a few lanterns, bathing the front of the store with their dull glow so he could see what was happening inside his store.

It was still difficult to see, though, and the shapes were moving about as people tried to run away from the snapping creatures, but at least now no one would be running into walls.

Looking about myself, I reached out and grabbed the first thing I thought I could use as a weapon, a piece of electrical conduit pipe.

In the front of the store, Fred and Norman were yelling, trying to gather people to them like army generals in a battle. A few listened, but most were running around like chickens with their heads cut off.

One of the creatures jumped onto the shelf next to me and its pincers came so close to my face I heard the click when they closed on empty air. Screaming in terror, I swung the pipe like a bat and knocked the thing away from me. It fell to the floor and landed on its back. Its multiple legs were twitching and then it righted itself, ready to resume the attack.

I didn't wait for it to launch itself again, but ran at it with the pipe over my head. I slammed it down onto its head and was greeted by a solid crunch when the carapace caved in. Yellow blood shot out and I danced away, knowing what would happen if that goo touched me.

A flash of fire from my right caused me to look to see what was happening and I was surprised to see it was the old woman, Judith. She didn't resemble the matron-like woman I had met earlier in the day, now she seemed like an avenging angel. She was holding two cans of Raid, one in each hand and when one was empty; she dropped it, pulled a cigarette lighter from a pocket, ignited the Raid and began spraying the creatures around her with the liquid napalm she had created. Squeals of alien pain filled the store and the smell of charred meat came to my nose.

One of the old men, I couldn't tell which one in the dark, but I thought it was Buddy, had one of the creatures in his hands, keeping the thing away from him. The pincers were snapping at his face and the man barely managed to fend the creature off with Fred's help. It dropped behind the counter and then I saw the two men stomping their feet. I assumed they were crushing the creature to mush.

I looked up to see Norman climbing onto the counter, his shotgun in his hand. The old man was yelling something, and when he leveled the shotgun into the depths of the store aisles, looking for targets, I knew we were all in danger.

"Michelle, get down. Now!" I yelled to her and she dropped to the floor just as Norman fired his first shot. I followed her and fell to the floor hard, not wanting to be hit by a stray round. In the shadows,

I didn't know if Norman had shot anything, but I knew the chances of him shooting either me, Kyle or Michelle was very good.

There was more shrieking and terror-filled screams as we all tried to battle the monstrosities attacking us. Looking back, the only reason any of us survived was because of their size, the vent limiting what could enter the store.

An ear piercing scream caused me to look to my left and I felt my blood run cold. Four of the scorpion creatures had found the young married couple and had swarmed over the young woman. The husband was valiantly trying to save her, but in his passion to save his wife; he wasn't watching his back. While he was kicking at the creature that was on top of his wife's head, three more came out of the darkness behind him and jumped onto his shoulders from behind. Their pincers dove deep, slashing his back to bloody ribbons and a second later he fell on top of his twitching wife.

After that, all I could see was the writhing pile of creatures as they swarmed over their prey.

Michelle cried out and I spun to see three more of them cornering her at the far end of the aisle. She had been slowly moving backwards, trying to stay away from those razor-sharp pincers. Kyle was in her arms, crying for his mommy and I knew I needed to act fast.

With my pipe in my hands, I called out to Bob who was a few feet away. He turned at my call and ran to me.

"Over there, my son and Michelle," I said in gasping syllables. Bob nodded, swung the pitchfork in his hands and charged the creatures, with me right behind him.

He was like something out of a barbarian movie, swinging the pitchfork high overhead like a warrior out of history. When he reached the first creature, he slammed the pitchfork down, the tines of the tool slicing into the carapace and cracking it open. The thing twitched on the end of the pitchfork and Bob tossed it away, the creature sliding off the end to slide down the smooth linoleum like a shuffleboard piece. Then he was at the second one, puncturing it in the ass and dragging it away from Michelle's legs. That left the last one for me and I charged it, only thinking about saving my son. I used the pipe like a spear and the inch round end punctured the creature right in the middle of its segmented body. It reared up, pincers trying to bite me around my waist and I recoiled instinctively, making a C with my body. It wasn't dead, but it wasn't moving that fast as I now had it trapped by the pipe, speared like a shish kabob. I noticed as it struggled that it weighed more than it looked, as if its body was somehow denser.

I wasn't as strong as Bob and it was a little harder for me to try and drag it away from Michelle, but I think all the adrenalin pumping in my system helped because, with a yell of terror and anger, I heaved my arms and actually lifted the creature off the floor, flinging it across the aisle to land on a shelf filled with light bulbs and wall outlets.

"You okay?" I asked in shuddering breaths.

Michelle nodded; her eyes as wide as large coins. I didn't blame her, I was so scared I thought I would die, too.

Another shotgun blast rang out and I ducked instinctively, but the blast came from the opposite end of the store. Bob was gone, helping someone else I assumed, and I took Michelle's hand, knowing we needed to get back to the front of the store and next to Norman, so we wouldn't get shot.

Another blast filled the store, mixing with the screams and cries around me. I had never fought in a war and never wanted to, but as people screamed for help around me, gunshots blared and blood pooled on the floor, I thought this must be what it would be like to be knee deep in battle.

I didn't like it at all.

Staying low, Michelle and I ran down the aisle, Kyle screaming he wanted to go home. When I reached the electrical department again, I grabbed another piece of conduit, as the first one had served me well.

When I reached the front of the store, I could see Judith again. The old woman was still using the aerosol cans as a makeshift flamethrower and I was impressed with her ingenuity, until one of the creatures attacked her from behind, slicing at her exposed ankles. She went down hard and her wrist twisted and the flame of the can was turned on her. In seconds, her dress was on fire and she was screaming, batting at the flames with her hands. The creatures never hesitated; diving at her while she tried to put herself out. She was a flaming torch and I truly believe it was almost a mercy when one of the creatures dove in and sliced her jugular with one of its pincers. Blood spurted out to extinguish some of the flames on her upper body and the entire store filled with the smell of burnt blood. Michelle couldn't stop her gag reflex and she leaned over and threw up, keeping her face away from Kyle. I believe I was still in shock from everything happening to really feel much of anything.

Another gunshot rang out, and a few feet away, two of the creatures disappeared in an explosion of shell and grey tissue. Looking around me, I saw Fred, and we made eye contact. He waved to me and I grabbed Michelle by the hand and pulled her along behind me. One of the creatures came at me and I kicked it hard in the head then whacked it with the pipe. It skittered away to look for easier prey.

Fred pointed up at the vent, where more of the creatures were still coming inside the store.

"We need to block that off or they'll never stop coming in here!" Fred yelled at me, his eyes wide with fear.

"So, what the hell do you want me to do about it?"

He handed me a cordless drill, a box of screws, and a piece of wood salvaged from one of the shelves behind the counter.

"I want you to block that vent off before we're all smothered under these things. I'm too damn old to be climbing up there!"

Ted was nearby and he was watching Fred's back, swiping at the creatures with a long street broom. He didn't hurt them, but it kept them at bay.

I looked to Michelle, her eyes filled with fear and she nodded.

"Go, he's right, John. Plug that hole before more get inside." One came close and she screamed, hugging Kyle tightly and Ted swept it away. Across the store, Bob now had a heavy metal shovel and he was running around, whacking the things one at a time. With each blow there was one less of the small creatures alive and the floor steamed with burning acid.

I took the drill and wood, shoving a handful of screws into my pocket, then ran over to the front window There was a display for sinks and toilets just under the vent and I began climbing on this, the whole giant shelving unit weaving from my weight.

But I managed to make it to the top without falling, and as I balanced precariously on top of a vanity sink selling for the low price of $99.99, I reached up and pushed the vent flap closed just as another of the creatures was coming through. Its head began to push at the flap and it took all of my strength to keep it from coming through. I had no weight behind me, my body standing on the sink. One good shove would send me toppling into space.

With my hand pressing the flap closed and holding the drill, I slammed the wood against the flap. Don't ask me how I managed to climb the shelf with the wood and drill because I barely remembered. I knew I would set something down, then climb higher and then transfer the item above me.

I could still feel the creature pressing on the flap and I carefully reached into my pocket to find a screw while my other hand held the wood in place and the drill. It was dark near the ceiling and I was going mostly by feel. There was more pressing on the vent and I assumed there were more of the creatures in there, all lined up and pushing as they waited for their chance to enter the hardware store.

The first three screws fell from my hands and tumbled to the floor as I tried to place them against the wood, but the fourth worked, the powerful, cordless drill sinking the screw perfectly. With one screw in, the pressure on the vent decreased and I hastily reached for another one. It took two more tries before I managed to get the drill and the screw together and the next screw went into the wood and the plaster underneath.

Now the pressure was gone, but I still made sure to sink three more screws into the wood at each corner and another on the bottom for the hell of it. Then I was out of screws and knew it was time to get back down. At first I tried to climb down with the drill in my hand and realized what an idiot I was being. Looking below me, I saw one of the things go near Michelle and I threw the drill at it. I only managed to graze it, but it was enough to distract it long enough so Ted could swoop in and push it away.

I continued climbing down, expecting to feel the sharp pincers of one of the things on my back at any second.

When I landed on the floor, I moved back to Fred. Norman was still on the counter, reloading the shotgun. Below him, was Carl, the old man I still didn't know, Michelle and Kyle. Ted was still sweeping creatures away and Bob was running around the store like a madman, whacking creatures like he was playing Whack-A-Mole.

I couldn't see where anyone else was, the smoke from Judith's body filling the store and the shadows almost complete. But the screaming had lessened and I didn't know yet if that was a good thing. The sound of Bob's shovel clanging on the floor became the predominant noise, and after five more minutes, even that subsided as the attacking things were slowly destroyed.

Norman shot the remaining ones near Ted, sending the carapaces in all directions. Droplets of yellow blood steamed everywhere, leaving small craters and pitted holes. Ted cried out once when a few drops of sprayed yellow ichor landed on his upper thigh, but he would live. There was one final crack of the shovel and then things seemed to quiet down, with the exception of muffled sobbing and cries of pain.

"Where's Willy, where's my grandson?' Norman called out and he swung the shotgun around in a circle.

"Now, hold on there, Norman, we'll find him. But first we need to make sure all those little bastards are dead," Fred said, while his eyes roamed the store. He was holding a pipe wrench in his hand, but hadn't used it; Norman keeping him safe.

Bob came out of the far right aisle, breathing hard and dragging the shovel behind him. Norman spun around and almost fired at Bob, but stopped himself in the nick of time. He was jumpy. Hell, we all were!

"You see my grandson back there?" Norman asked.

Bob was covered in sweat and there were dozens of small spots where the spraying blood from smashed creatures had peppered him. He shook his head no and plopped down on one of the stools near the counter.

"I think I got them all," he said in a hoarse voice.

Another cry of anguish filled the store and we all looked in the direction we thought it came from. Looking around, I saw we were missing more people and I took a step forward, then stopped and turned to Michelle.

"I want to go see if anyone's hurt. You'll be okay?"

She nodded that she would be.

Kyle was still crying and he reached for me. I decided an extra second wouldn't matter and I took my son, hugging him tightly.

"I want to go home, Daddy, right now! I don't want to see the monsters anymore. I want to go see Mommy, she needs us!" He said all this into my neck as he hugged me with his small arms.

Rubbing the back of his shirt and feeling his shoulder blades beneath, I was once again reminded of how fragile he was.

"And we will, sport, I promise; just a little while longer."

"But I want to go now!" He cried, his shoulders shaking as he sobbed into my neck, his tears moistening my shirt. With a weary sigh, I peeled him off me, not wanting to let go, but knowing there were things to do, distasteful things, such as the body of Judith that was still smoldering in the middle of the store.

"Here, take him, I'll be back in a few minutes," I told Michelle and turned to Ted and Bob. "You guys want to give me a hand checking out the store?"

They both nodded they would, Bob picking the shovel up and holding it next to him. Ted stuck with the broom; it had served him well thus far.

"What about you, Carl, you want to come help us?" I asked.

Carl shook his head emphatically, no. "I'll stay here with Fred and Norman, if it's all the same to you," he said.

I grinned despite the present situation. "Wouldn't have expected it any other way, Carl." Then I turned from him, dismissing him as the coward he was. Fred handed me an oil lantern and I thanked him with a nod.

With Ted and Bob at my side, we moved into the shadows of the store to try and see who was still alive and who wasn't.

10

CONFRONTATION

CASUALTIES

WITH ME IN the lead, we all moved into the darkening shadows of the hardware store with two purposes in mind. The first was to make sure all the creatures had been killed, and the second was to find any survivors. At the present moment, I only knew Judith was dead, as to the other people in the store, I could only guess. Bob was on my right and Ted my left, holding the lantern out like an innkeeper calling people in from a storm. The alien bodies were everywhere, legs sticking up in the air like dry twigs. A few still shuddered when we approached them and Bob slammed the shovel on them, finishing the job he'd started.

If there were any more of the foul creatures in the store, they were hiding, and I didn't believe they were that intelligent. All they knew was to hunt, and I don't think they would even consider laying in wait for an unwary person to pass them from the shadows of the store shelves.

We found Willy first near the far left corner of the store. He was sprawled out on the floor, his limbs at odd angles. Ted leaned down close to his face and we all backed away a step at the sight of his swollen, bloated features. He resembled a massive balloon now, all of his body swollen to the point of bursting. Four of the creatures lay near him and a hammer was two feet from his right hand.

Though the things had gotten him in the end, he had fought valiantly. We stared down at his body, and I thought about what I was going to tell Norman, when suddenly, Willy's face seemed to move in the light of the lantern.

"Wait a second, Ted, bring the light closer, there's something wrong with his face."

"You mean besides being dead? Poor bastard," he said, but complied with my request. When the light was only a foot or so away from Willy's face, I could see the flesh was undulating like a living thing. His eyes were closed, but his eyelids were moving, fluttering like he was sleeping, deep in REM sleep, his eyeballs moving about under the lids. His cheeks seemed to expand and then contract and his throat began to move up and down like he was trying to swallow something that just wouldn't go down.

"What the fuck is wrong with him?" Bob asked while staring at the swollen, vibrating face of the pimple-faced teenager.

I was about to say I had absolutely no idea when the skin on Willy's cheeks split open, his eyes peeled back, and his throat spilt apart like a dagger had sliced him from the inside.

I gasped in utter shock when the first small pincers poked out of the tear in his throat and moved back and forth as if they were smelling the air. No sooner did the first pair of pincers pop out, then a hundred more appeared, flowing out of the body to cover it like a carpet. They were no larger than a full grown ant, but as I knew from experience, they would grow to epic proportions.

The small scorpion-creatures didn't notice us, but instead began consuming the body from the outside in, burrowing back into the flesh. Willy's face began to sink into itself and his chest and stomach began to collapse like a deflated water bottle as the small carnivores digested him.

"Jesus Christ, will you look at that?" Ted whispered while he held the light over the corpse. The light was flickering, thanks to Ted now having the shakes.

The light gave the grotesque sight an even more macabre look as the small creatures swarmed over the body like an ant colony.

Then I snapped out of my stupor, realizing that once these things were done feeding, they would spread out into the store and we would never find them all. No sooner did I think this then Bob was at my side. I hadn't realized he had left me. Before I could ask him what we should do, he raised his left hand and squirted an entire can of charcoal lighter fluid onto the corpse. Some of the tiny creatures squirmed in what appeared to be pain, but most were unharmed by the lighter fluid.

With out hesitating, Bob pulled a book of matches from his pocket, flicked a match and lit it, dropping the small flame onto the body.

There was a whoosh and the body began to burn, the small creatures curling into balls from the heat. Was it my imagination or did I hear small squeals of pain, like when we had killed that dog-sized one in the back room? The fire hissed and smoked and in less than five minutes time the body was a blackened husk, only a few flames still burning here and there. The odor of charred meat filled the store yet again to hover near the ceiling, and I wondered what the others were thinking back at the counter.

A few of the tiny creatures tried to escape the flames, but we quickly stepped on them, looking for all purposes like a bunch of kids stomping on ants in springtime.

"Better go tell them we're all right back here, but don't say who we found to Norman, at least not yet," I said to Ted. "And be careful."

"Hell, yes, I will," Ted said and took off back down the aisle. There was light from the flames of the body, so Bob and I could still see. Bob walked a few feet away and came back with one of those tiki lamps people would place around the picnic table so they could see at night during outside parties. He lowered the lamp to the flames and the torch caught after the second try. He stood next to me in the wan, flickering light of the torch, shovel in one hand, torch in the other. I thought it would suit him perfectly if he ripped off his shirt and blackened his face, he looked so wild.

Footsteps sounded from behind me and first the light of the

lantern appeared bouncing up and down, then Ted appeared behind it.

"All set, I told them we had to burn some stuff, I didn't say what, though. Norman's antsy to find his grandson."

"Yeah, well, he won't be in a little while. Come on, let's keep going, there's still others around here somewhere," I added.

We called out, but there were no answers and we continued moving through the aisles. I had never really given it much thought, but the hardware store was quite big.

Especially in the dark. The building was like a massive tomb with no windows, with the exception of the plate-glass front wall to let in natural light. There were no skylights either. The building had been built so many years ago; conservation had barely been a word.

Two aisles over, we came upon the next casualties of the creatures. It was the young married couple. Both were ripped to shreds, almost all of their flesh gone. If it wasn't for the tattered remains of their clothing, I don't even think I could have identified them. Ted leaned the lantern close to the bodies, but the skin remained immobile. For whatever reason, these two unfortunate people were used for food, while Willy had been used for gestation. Bob took a plastic bag from the shelf nearby, ripped it open and laid it over the two bodies. We would be back for them soon enough, but first we needed to check the rest of the aisles.

We moved through the aisles until we came upon the back of the store. None of us realized we weren't alone until four shadows moved out of the darkness to surround us, makeshift weapons pointed at us. I also saw a small handgun aimed at me so I raised my hands in surrender.

"Whoa, now guys, easy does it," I said. "We're just checking on everyone to see who's still with us."

Grille spit onto the floor as he waved a large pipe he'd taken from the plumbing department at my face.

"Well, we're fine, so fuck off," he growled. Behind him and the others, an oil lantern sat on a plastic bucket. In the dim light of their lantern and Ted's, I was able to see there were more than a dozen of those creatures spread out on the floor, all very dead.

"Did you kill all those?" I asked, gesturing to the broken bodies.

"Hell yeah, we did. Smashed those bastards up good. Why, what's it to you?"

Bob moved in, his hand tight on the shovel's handle. "Why? Because we could have used your help a little while ago, that's why. You stayed here and guarded your own ass while people were dying!" By the time he had finished, his last words were almost screams.

Grille didn't seem to care. "So fuckin' what? Me and my boys don't give a shit about you white pricks. You can all go screw yourselves for all we care."

"Probably already did, that blonde bitch is fine," This came from Quick who grinned widely in the shadows. The other two men chuckled and Grille flashed his steel teeth, the light reflecting off it like crystal.

I knew they were talking about Michelle, but I knew better than to say anything. Men like these four were only effective if you let them think they were getting to you.

"Look, just get the fuck out of here, all right? We don't need your help," Grille barked, waving his hand in the air. "Once this shit is over and the sun comes back, we are so gone."

Bob was about to say something in reply when I stopped him.

"Forget it, Bob, let them be, please. We've got more problems than those guys to worry about."

Bob made a show of not listening, like he was going to punch Grille in the mouth, despite the small handgun aimed at him. Slim had it tucked close to his body, protecting it, knowing it could be knocked out of his outstretched hand if he had stretched his arm out.

"Fine, let's go," Bob said, staring Grille down.

Grille chuckled heartfully. "Yeah, that's right, Hercules, start walking and don't come back." His cronies all laughed and went back to whatever they were doing before we arrived, laughing about how they kicked our white asses away from them. Bob was stewing, but I slowly got him to calm down, explaining that they would get what's coming to them in the end. That if we didn't stick together, we would all surely die. Ted agreed with me and Bob slowly relaxed. When we turned the next aisle and saw the two gay men laying side by side on the floor, Bob had forgotten all about the gangbangers. At first we thought both men were dead, but then Jordan looked up at us and we realized he was definitely alive.

"Help me, please, it's Shaun, he's not breathing anymore," Jordan said, tears creasing the blood on his cheeks.

We ran then, crossing the distance in less than a second and Bob and I dropped down next to the two prone men. Ted hovered nearby casting the lantern's glow over us so we could see. We were in the far right corner of the hardware store now, about as far as we could get from the counter.

I gently helped Jordan sit up and moved him so his back was against a shelf full of potting soil. The bags crinkled as Jordan's weight pressed against them. A few of the bags had been ripped open and the dirt had spilled onto the floor. Blood from Jordan, Shaun, or both, had soaked into the dirt to make a thick, black slurry.

While I moved Jordan, Bob checked Shaun, but it took him less than a minute to find that the man was dead. Even without checking for a pulse, the ragged gash in his throat where his jugular was would be proof enough.

"What happened?" I asked. But I already had an idea. There were about seven or eight of the creatures around Jordan in multiple pieces and a pair of bloody, scored hedge clippers at his feet. He had killed them all single handedly.

"We were lying down together," Jordan was saying in ragged gasps. The man was in shock, no doubt about it. "We figured we'd come over here so no one would see us. Most people are uncomfortable around us. Because of the fact we're gay. I've learned to brush it off, but Shaun has a hard time with it. He cared what people thought of him, even complete strangers. We were sleeping when we heard a yell and then those things dropped down from the ceiling. One landed right on his face and it cut into his throat. He couldn't talk and I think he choked on his own blood. I grabbed the thing and tossed it away from him, but his throat was cut too bad. I fought the others that attacked us and then went to help Shaun." He held up his hand, covered in sticky blood. "I tried to hold his wound closed, but the blood just seeped out of the sides of my hand."

I didn't know what to say, so I said nothing. Bob had closed Shaun's eyes so the dead man now appeared to be sleeping. Jordan looked into my eyes and the tears began again.

"Why did this have to happen? Was it God? Is it because we're gay? I loved him and now he's gone." He began crying then, and not knowing what to do, I leaned forward and hugged this poor man. Jordan hugged me back, his head against my chest, and he cried, great shuddering sobs that filled the aisle around us. Neither Bob nor Ted said a thing, but merely stayed next to us.

I patted Jordan's back and rocked and hugged him like I would my son, saying soothing words to make him feel better; hoping in some small way they might penetrate his sadness and do just that.

Thinking of my wife at home, my parents in Andover, and my sister in New Hampshire, somewhere out there in the darkness; I felt my own tears well up inside me. But I forced them down, not wanting to cry in front of Bob and Ted. There was really no reason I should feel this way. I'm sure neither man would have looked at me any differently if I did begin to cry. Lord only knows we've all seen enough so we should all be nothing but gibbering idiots by now.

But I held it back, thinking if I opened those floodgates, I just might not be able to stop. So with Jordan sobbing in my arms, weeping uncontrollably, unafraid of showing us, mere strangers, his sadness and loss, I wondered if he wasn't a braver man than me.

11

BURYING THE DEAD

CONTEMPLATION

NORMAN DIDN'T TAKE the news about Willy very well.

He sat down behind the counter and his face went slack, his jaw falling open and tears sliding down his cheeks. The other older man I didn't know (but I asked Fred and found out his name was Reuben), and Buddy, stayed with Norman, trying their best to console the man.

No one expected their consoling to help, but at least Norman wasn't alone with his grief. Reuben had known Willy as well and also mourned the teenager's death.

I went to Kyle and Michelle and hugged them both, Kyle falling into my arms and squeezing me tightly. He had been crying again and after a while of sitting with him, rocking him back and forth like I had Jordan, he fell back to sleep. It was almost three in the morning and everyone was still exhausted, but we all agreed we wouldn't sleep until all the corpses and the creatures carcasses were out of the main store.

With Ted, Fred, Bob and Earl to help, the five of us began the gruesome duty of picking up the bodies and bringing them to the back room. Carl watched us walking away and I almost went over and grabbed the man by the scruff of his shirt and dragged him with us, but I decided what would be the point. The man was useless and it was a damn shame that so many good people were dead and that coward was still breathing. Jordan wanted to help, too, but I told him to just rest, that we would treat Shaun's body with respect, and we did.

Buddy knew the store as well as Norman, having spent many years hanging around the counter to pass the time, and he knew where there was a dolly. With the metal cart, it was a lot easier to move the bodies. Two of us would grab an end of each corpse and then set the body on the dolly, then another would wheel it to the rear room, where two more of us were ready to unload it. We did this three times, doubling up twice with the bodies on the dolly, and when we were done, we had quite the pile of corpses.

All the corpses were piled next to and on top of Peter, and I wondered if the man's soul was glad for the company.

Bob, with Ted's help, spread another, larger tarp across the top of the pile and then we all stood silent for a moment, each sending a silent prayer for our lost comrades to find whatever Heaven they believed in.

It was a poor grave for those people, but it was the best we could do at the moment. I wondered what would happen in a few days when the bodies began to decompose. I wondered about the smell and how bad it would get.

I had been on a walk one day about a year ago and it had been a beautiful summer day. As I rounded a corner, I was assaulted by an aroma that almost knocked me off my feet. It is really hard to describe in words what it smelled like. I guess someone would have to experience the aroma for themselves to really know what I'm describing, but when I turned the corner, there was a large, dead cat lying in the gutter with most of its insides leaking out. It had been dead for more than a day and it was pulsating with maggots as they squirmed about inside its body cavity, and the odor of decomposing meat was overwhelming. It was like a wall had hit you in the face and would knock you over if you weren't careful. The redolence was so bad it was almost suffocating, and the only reason I stopped myself from vomiting was because I was able to get by the dead animal quickly and was back in the fresh air of the day before my stomach gave up the small control I was able to maintain.

But what would happen inside the store when all those human bodies began to rot?

Trying not to think about it, I left the back room with the others, Buddy taking care of the dolly. He wiped it down with some bleach and used a few rags lying about in the back room. We all thanked him, but told him it was probably unnecessary. Why would we need the dolly again unless it was to transport more bodies? He didn't answer us, but continued working. I think he just wanted to do something; to complete a task he had control over. Everyone deals with stress in different ways, and Buddy wanted to clean the dolly, thereby taking control of his life in some small way.

Cleaning up the bodies and dead creatures went smooth except for one time.

When we moved Willy's body, the four gangbangers came over to us. They wouldn't help us, but they had plenty to say to us, calling us names and just trying to aggravate us in general. No one took the bait, which I was glad for, and we all tried to ignore them. Only once, when Bob was walking by Grille did I think something was going to happen. Bob had a temper on the best of days and I was impressed that the man had managed to stay calm for so long already.

Grille tried everything, including attacking Bob's ancestry and his wife, which we were all sure he didn't know personally. But in the end, Bob had turned the other cheek and we all told him he did the right thing. Bob gave us a face that said he wasn't so sure.

Once all the bodies were cleaned up, we set to cleaning up the small scorpion-like creatures. We used pitchforks and rakes and soon had them all in plastic garbage bags, double bagged for safety. A few holes appeared in the plastic, the yellow blood eating through the bags, but it appeared after the things were dead for a while, the blood would lose almost all of its potency. We dragged the bags to the back room and dumped them in a corner.

After leaving the back room for the second time, we all went our separate ways, most congregating near the counter. I wasn't ready to go back and talk to Michelle and the others, so I wandered over to the front double doors of the store. More lanterns were on and more torches were lit, banishing the shadows to the far corners of the store. I heard Ted and Bob talking and Fred was already organizing a few people to try and clean up some of the blood pooling on the floor with sawdust and potting soil. Halfway to the doors, I heard Fred tell Carl to help and thought the skinny man protested, but Bob made sure he didn't protest for long.

Good, I thought, make the little coward do some work for a change. So far, the only thing he'd contributed was that he had a weak bladder and had seen the creatures come in through the vent. Hell, Kyle could have done that if he'd been awake.

I stopped at the glass doors and tried to peer outside, but all I was greeted to was utter darkness. Cupping my hands to the glass, I tried to block out any inside light, and once my eyes adjusted, I was surprised to see I could actually see a few feet from the doors. I stared for a few minutes and then I saw my first creature. It was one of the scorpion things and it skittered in front of the doors on its multiple feet. This one was large, as big as a Doberman Pincher and I made sure to stay perfectly still as it trundled past the doors. It was gone in less than a minute and I turned my head to follow it, but it was lost from sight, swallowed up by the dark void once again. I continued to stare out the doors and after a while I could have sworn I could see the first few cars parked near the front of the building. Squinting and cupping my hands tighter, I was almost positive I could see Fred's jeep.

I was about to pull away and tell Fred how his jeep really wasn't that far away, when another shape in the darkness appeared near the jeep. It was only there for a second, and I really couldn't make it out that well, but I had the impression of something that looked like a giant bat, only this creature was as large as a compact car. That made me think some more about those creatures out there in the darkness and my heart began to race. So far, I'd only seen scorpion creatures as big as large dogs, but could there be more that were even larger? How big did they grow? As big as a car? A house? Bigger? If they were bigger than what I'd seen so far, than sooner or later the hardware store would be a deathtrap. I believe the only reason the front plate-glass windows were left alone for as long as they were was because the creatures didn't understand how fragile the glass was compared to their strength.

And time was against us. We had been in the store for less than a day and we had already lost a quarter of our numbers. What would happen in two days? Three?

I believe it was at that moment, as I weighed the survival of myself, Kyle and the others, that I decided if we were going to live, we would need to get out of the hardware store.

The only question after that decision would be how do I convince the others to follow me? And then where exactly should we go?

12

COMFORT

I DON'T KNOW how long I stood at those glass doors and stared at the abyss outside, but eventually I turned away. On my way back to Michelle and Kyle I paused at the cash register.

Something had caught my eye.

It was a small box of pocket notebooks and a Boston Red Sox cup full of pens.

I don't know what possessed me to pick up two of the notebooks and take three ball-point pens, but I did. I was never much of a writer, in fact, in school, I always did terrible in creative writing, but this was different.

Something inside me wanted to write down what I had experienced and the people who had been with me. I felt I needed to record what was happening to me and my son. If anything, it was a way to let out what I was feeling in a constructive way.

I wasn't foolish enough to think anyone would ever find my words after I wrote them down, but I still felt I needed to do this, if for nothing else than to somehow take control of my own world, much like when Buddy had cleaned the dolly.

So, now armed with the pens and notebooks, I would begin writing all this down.

After slipping the notebooks and pens into my pocket, I returned to Michelle and Kyle. Kyle was still sleeping and I didn't blame him. The ordeal my son was suffering was enough to make me want to breakdown and cry. You want so badly to protect your children from evil, but sometimes, no matter how hard you try, evil forces its way into your world and all you can do is stand witness to it.

I slid down to the floor and Michelle reached out her hand to me. Without thinking about it, I took her hand and squeezed it.

"We're okay, you know. We're gonna be okay," I said to her, though looking back, I think I said it more for my benefit than hers.

She smiled back to me, her eyes twinkling in the gloom of the aisle and she nodded. "I know we will, John. With you watching out for us, how could it be any other way?"

We didn't talk after that, and she scooted over next to me and we sat together quietly. Behind us, near the counter, Fred could be heard talking in a soft voice as he tried to rationalize what was happening to them. That was how Fred was dealing with what had happened. He was trying to place reason on an unreasonable event. Whatever had happened to the sun and brought the strange creatures prowling around on the streets outside and attacking us in the store was beyond any of our minds. It was the stuff of fantasy made real and no matter how hard any of us tried to comprehend it, to try would simply drive us mad.

That was why I did my best not to think about what was happening to us; instead I tried to focus my attention on Kyle.

Reuben gathered candy bars and soda from the machines and shelves near the front door and distributed them amongst the groups. No one really ate, no matter how hungry we felt. It just didn't feel right. I think everyone was still on edge, but Norman was able to fill Fred and Bob in on any other vents or openings in the hardware store, and after making sure they were all secure, we were fairly confident we were safe from outside invasion. Luckily, there were no windows, the building frame made of solid, stone cinderblocks.

Kyle woke up after the first hour and munched on half a candy bar and drank an entire can of soda. He needed to go to the bathroom, so with a flashlight in hand, I escorted him to the rear restroom, where he quickly did his business and then ran out of the stall like there was a demon behind him. I didn't blame him; the bathroom was all oppressive, with only my flashlight to keep the shadows at bay. He ran into my arms and we quickly vacated the tile-covered room. I went by Carl and Buddy on my way back, the two men having to use the bathroom next. I nodded politely to Buddy, but I ignored Carl. Buddy had a grandfatherly look and he reminded me of my own grandfather who was dead for more than twenty years.

We settled back down again, and in less than ten minutes, with his stomach full and his bladder empty, Kyle drifted off into a restless slumber.

I sat there watching him quietly, wishing I could use my will alone to free him from this horrible nightmare. I could still hear voices around me as the others talked and debated about what was happening. While they chatted, I wrote in my notebook, trying to remember everything I had experienced and realizing I perhaps didn't want to remember. The entire time Michelle sat near me, at first staring at the ceiling and then down at Kyle.

Eventually, everyone stopped talking, and by the end of the second hour after the attack, after they had all sat down and rested, and the adrenaline filling their veins had long past, leaving them exhausted, they finally closed their eyes and rested, some slipping off into restless sleep filled with unsettling dreams.

Lanterns were turned down and candles were blown out so we could all rest, only a few nightlights still remaining on.

After the third hour, I grew weary of writing and found my own eyes were growing heavy and I laid down next to Michelle who had spread out on the floor next to Kyle a half hour ago.

Kyle was curled up in her arms as if she was his mother and I wasn't upset about seeing this. Michelle was playing the surrogate, standing in for Karen, and I thought that was a good thing right now. Kyle needed to know he was safe, and if something happened and I had to leave him, it was good to know he would feel safe with Michelle until I returned.

I lay there fully exhausted, staring at the back of Michelle's head and I found myself wanting her. I remembered the countless times we made love all those years ago and how our two bodies had meshed into one being, both in body and soul. Then I thought of Karen and I felt guilty for thinking such adulterous thoughts. But then Michelle would sigh in her sleep and I would find myself wanting her again.

I was so conflicted. I missed my wife terribly, but just as my son was frightened, so too was I. Just because I was an adult didn't mean I wouldn't want someone to hold me close and whisper into my ear that everything would be fine, that tomorrow everything would go back to normal. Even if those words would all be lies, I could still close my eyes and pretend, just for a little while, that I was safe.

I squeezed my eyes closed, trying to will myself to sleep, but now that I was laying in the dark, doing nothing; my mind was racing. I could feel my heart beating faster as I thought about the danger I was in; that my son was in.

A rustling of clothing caused me to open my eyes, and in the glow of the one lantern at the end of the aisle I looked into Michelle's face. She had turned over and was awake, her eyes seeming to peer into me, to see through me like she used to do when we would lay awake in the dark for hours and talk after making love.

"You sleeping?" She asked and shifted her arm to a more comfortable position. Behind her, Kyle rolled a foot away, still on the mattress of rags, and falls deeper into sleep. His breathing is quick and I know it's because he's exhausted and his body has finally fallen into that slumber that only a child can maintain. A sleep so deep it would take a bomb to wake him.

"No, not really. How 'bout you?" I said, staring into her eyes. We are alone in our aisle, the others spread out in the other aisles nearby.

"I slept a little, but you know…it's hard to rest while I'm thinking what could happen."

I nod my head, understanding completely

She takes her free hand and reaches out to me, touching my cheek, caressing my neck. I close my eyes and enjoy the touch of another human being. I want this, hell, I need this.

She leans forward hesitantly, her lips parting slightly and I do the same. Our lips touch in the darkness. And it all comes back to me, like the past ten-plus years had never happened. I kiss her long and deeply, my tongue exploring her mouth. Her smell fills me and it's like we're back in my bedroom again, my parents gone for the day. I reach out and pull her to me and we meld into one person, her warmth penetrating my clothing to my skin beneath.

But then I open my eyes and gently push her away, despite my body and my rock hard erection telling me different.

"No, wait, Michelle, I can't. Look, I still care for you, I never stopped caring, but I'm married now. I love my wife and I don't want to betray her."

She smiles slightly and nods her head and then she caresses my cheek again.

"Oh, John, sweet, noble John. I understand what you're saying, but have you even thought that for all you know, your wife is already dead? That you might be faithful to nothing but a memory? That maybe everyone else in the entire world is dead and this could be our last night on earth? That tonight could truly be our last chance together? And if so, don't we deserve that one last night of being together? To just hold one another and pretend everything is all right. I'm not trying to take you from your wife, John, but she isn't here and I am and I know I need to be held. Would you hold me, John, please? Would you tell me that this is all a crazy nightmare and that tomorrow I'll wake up in my bed with nothing but a fading memory of a bad dream? You and me isn't a betrayal, you know. We're just two people who need to be touched and it doesn't change a thing about the way you feel for your wife."

There are tears in her eyes now and I reach out and brush one away from her cheek with my thumb. I can't help myself and I lean forward and kiss her lips, tasting the salt of her tears. They're wet and sweet and I know that I love her. Even if tomorrow comes and the sun is back and my wife is fine and I never see Michelle again. Tonight I love her and I know I want to be with her. We kiss again and soon we are naked, rolling around in the rags as we make gentle, soft love. I climax twice and she at least the same as we lose ourselves in each others bodies. Though I know its Michelle in my arms and I caress her soft skin and round curves, I still can't help but close my eyes and pretend it's my wife, that it's Karen next to me, pressing her body against mine as I fall into a deep, exhausted sleep.

My last waking thought is a prayer for Karen. I pray to any god that will listen to look after her, to protect her, because sooner or later I'm going to return to her, even if I have to fight through every hellish creature waiting for me in the darkness beyond.

13

SHOOTOUT

I WAS AWOKEN the next morning, or what I thought was morning, by the sounds of arguing voices. Next to me, Michelle rolled over and breathed out a heavy sigh. Her eyes were still closed, and she was still fast asleep. Next to her, Kyle was still sleeping softly, as well. His head was now on Michelle's arm, and I thought the two looked just like mother and son.

For some reason that thought still didn't make me feel so unhappy.

More agitated voices came to me and I sat up, rubbing my face with my hands. Sometime in the night, after Michelle and I had made love for the third time, we took an extra second to redress, not wanting to give away our business to the others, but somehow I doubted if they were oblivious. The aisles weren't that big and I distinctly remember Michelle crying out in pleasure more than once.

I looked up when Bob dashed from around the end of the aisle and ran to me, his face creased with concern.

"We got problems," he said and crouched down next to me. His eyes drifted over Michelle's supine form but didn't linger. That made me worry. If Bob wasn't interested in Michelle's curves then something must be bad.

"What is it? Are more of those things inside the store?" I asked this as my heart began to race. Already my eyes were darting around me, looking at the shelves, trying to find a weapon.

Bob shook his head back and forth. "No, it's not those things, but it might be just as bad." He looked up, over and beyond me and then back down, making sure the aisle was still clear. "It's those four black guys. They want some food and Norman isn't happy about it. He told them to go straight to Hell. That it's his store and if they don't like it they can leave. Now there's some kind of a standoff. They said they aren't leaving the front of the store without food."

Michelle was awake now, and she had lain there next to me, listening quietly.

"What do the others say?" She asked; the first sign I had that she was awake and listening to the conversation.

Bob looked down at her. "They don't have an opinion. It is Norman's store after all and if he doesn't want to give those guys his food who are we to say different?" Bob looked me square in the face and I could see the worry in his eyes. There was something he wasn't telling me. As if he sensed this, Bob spoke.

"Norman's waving his shotgun at them and he says if they don't go back to the rear of the store and leave him alone he's gonna shoot Grille, then the rest."

That did it. All we needed was Norman shooting people he didn't agree with, even if those same people were assholes. Plus, now was not the time to argue amongst ourselves. We all needed to pull together to fight the common enemy, namely the creatures in the dark. Internal squabbling would only hurt us. I told most of this to Bob and he nodded, agreeing with me.

"Yeah, I know that, and though those guys are jerks, they are tough. They took out almost a dozen of those monsters all by themselves last night. They can handle themselves. We need them with us. Norman isn't making that easy, but..." He shrugged. "It is his hardware store."

I was on my feet now, sliding my feet into my sneakers and then tying them quickly as I glanced down at Michelle.

"Will you watch Kyle for me?"

She nodded. "Of course, just be careful."

Our eyes made contact and I held her gaze for a moment longer than I needed to. A lot was said to each other in that moment.

"I will. If you hear trouble, just stay down and wait until you hear the all clear from me or Bob."

"All right," she answered, her hand going to Kyle's back and rubbing him in a motherly way. There was that image again. I gazed down at Kyle, still fast asleep, and pulled my eyes away.

Looking at Bob, I slapped him on the arm. "Okay, let's go see what we can do to stop this shit before it boils over."

Bob nodded, and with him in the lead, we moved down the aisle towards the counter, the voices still arguing back and forth in anger.

* * *

When I look back on what happened next, it all seems like a dream. Everything happened so fast it would take time for me to process the experience. Even now, as I write this all down, I still wonder if I'm getting it all correct. In the shadows of the store, with bodies moving around, I think I pieced a lot of it together, some through assumptions, but this is what I remember and I guess that's all that really matters in the end.

Bob exited the aisle and raised his hand for me to stop. I moved up next to him, but didn't try to pass. To our right was the counter.

Norman was standing behind it, and in the dim glow of the lantern, it was easy to see the polished metal of his shotgun. He was pointing the barrel down into the store and I couldn't see what he was looking at or who he was talking to. Bob gestured for me to follow him and we both crossed the lane and stopped by the checkout aisle, the cash register sitting contently, waiting for the next customer.

From this new vantage point, I was now able to see the front of the store better and could see who Norman was talking to.

Grille stood with his three cronies behind him and was waving a knife in the air in a very threatening gesture.

"Come on, old man, we're hungry. It's been almost a day and we haven't had any food; just the damn water from the sink in the bathroom. Give us some of that candy you got from those machines.

We got money if we have to pay for them." Grille used the tip of the knife to point to the machines and then back to the pile of candy bars on the counter

Norman shook his white head of hair and scowled deeply. "I don't want your damn money, you piece of shit. These candy bars are for me and my customers. They're for all of us that are in this together and that ain't you, so fuck off and go back to your hole in the back of my store."

"Screw that, old man, we want some of that food and if you won't give it to us then we'll take it." This came from Big Louie who stood just to the left of Grille. Slim and Quick nodded their heads in agreement.

"What about the rest of you people?" Grille asked, looking at Fred, Ted, Carl and the others. "Are you just gonna let us starve? Hell, man, we're people, too. We deserve to eat."

"You don't deserve jack, now this is your last warning. Get out of here and go to the back of the store or I'm gonna shoot your damn fool head off." Norman pumped the shotgun to prove his point and Grille took a step backward, as did the others. What I didn't know at the time, but would find out a few minutes later, was that Slim had backed away from Grille and into the shadows, and was now circling around to the other side of the counter, flanking Norman. While Grille kept Norman occupied, Slim moved closer to the old man, staying just in the shadows and out of sight.

Grille raised his arm at Norman in a threatening gesture, the knife in his hand reflecting the glow of the oil lantern, the tip pointing directly at Norman's chest. "This is your last chance, you old fossil. Give us some of that candy or this is gonna go bad."

Norman's jaw set and he raised the shotgun. "Goddammit, you no good punk, this is my store and no one tells me what to do in my store."

Grille seemed to smile then, but looking back, now I think it was more of a sneer. His knife was high in the air in the palm of his hand, and I think when he lowered it, that was the signal for Slim to fire the small .22 he was holding.

There was the tiny pop of the small handgun and a small flash of light as the bullet exited the muzzle. A half-second later, the bullet found its mark in Norman's right shoulder.

I don't know if Norman fired the shotgun because he wanted to or because of the shock of being shot himself, but his finger squeezed the trigger and the shotgun roared; the full blast taking Grille low in the chest. The gangbanger went down hard onto his back, falling between Quick and Big Louie who seemed to be as shocked as the rest of us. Something I thought of before when I first met these men came back, that sometimes it was all for show and in truth perhaps these men were really no different from me or any of us trapped inside the hardware store.

Grille's head struck the floor and the sound of a cracking skull could be heard, like the dry snap of a finger sized branch. Not that it mattered. Grille's lower chest cavity was a bloody, open wound that spilled blood onto the floor. Some of his intestines were exposed and had slipped out of the cavity while Grille's mouth spewed a bloody froth into the air to patter back onto his face. He choked once; gagging on his own bile, then went still.

Everyone in the store who had a view of what was happening stared at the mutilated body of Grille, but no sooner did my eyes take in the fallen gangbanger then another blast filled the store.

Norman had figured out where Slim was and had turned, firing again, striking Slim in the neck just as the skinny gangbanger fired his handgun for the second time. The shot went wide, disappearing into the darkness as the man screamed in agony. Half the man's neck, and a good part of his face disappeared in a spray of blood, and Slim sank to the floor like one of those blow-up Holiday decorations people put on their lawn on Christmas and Halloween when they're unplugged for the night.

"Jesus Christ, Norman, what the hell are you doing?" Fred asked in a shocked voice as he ducked low to the floor, scared of getting shot.

Norman never looked away from the two remaining gangbangers.

"I'm protecting what's mine, that's what," he said in an almost casual tone. He swung the barrel of the shotgun back to Big Louie and Quick. Blood seeped from the wound on Norman's shoulder, staining his shirt crimson. The blood looked black in the shadows cast by the oil lantern, but the man barely noticed.

Quick realized he was staring death in the face and raised his hands in front of his body, screaming for Norman not to shoot.

"No, please, man, don't kill me! It was Grille's idea, all of it, please, don't!" But the last words were muffled by another roar of the shotgun. Quick's hands disappeared in a red mist as the buckshot ripped them off and then continued into the man's upper chest. Quick was thrown back into the shadows, and in the reverberating echo of the gunshot, I could hear the man's death-rattle.

Norman wasn't through yet. He had decided to clean house and there was one more rat in the cellar.

He swung the shotgun to Big Louie and prepared to fire, but the large man, belaying his size, ran straight for the double glass door at the front of the store.

Norman hesitated, knowing the target was not getting away and let the big gangbanger run for his life.

Big Louie charged for the doors, I expect his back itching as he expected a load of buckshot to penetrate his body at any moment, but it didn't come.

Reaching the double doors, the man turned back to look at Norman and the rest of us. He scanned each of our faces, looking for mercy, but found none.

Norman gestured with the muzzle of the shotgun for Big Louie to get going.

"Go on, boy, get or I'll fill you full of lead." Norman aimed the shotgun at his head to illustrate his point.

Big Louie said nothing, but unlocked the double doors and ran into the outer darkness that had become our world. The second he was through the doors, I saw Ted charge after him, but he wasn't going after the man; he was running to the doors to lock them again.

I ran after him, wanting to see if I could see Big Louie. Upon reaching the glass, I placed my hands against it and peered into the blackness. There he was, walking slowly near Fred's Jeep. I could see him because he had a small flashlight in his hand, probably taken from one of the store's shelves.

"He looks okay," Ted said as we watched together.

"Yeah, so far," I added. But then I saw a few of the scorpion creatures moving about behind Big Louie. Some of them were cat-sized, but I saw a few others the size of large dogs. I swallowed hard. There was a knot in my throat that wouldn't go away.

The man didn't have that much time left. But the time I thought he had was cut even shorter a second later.

The flashlight was bobbing up and down as Big Louie tried to figure out where to go. Then a shape appeared above him. It was impossible to see the full image of what was in the dark, but thanks to the flashlight, I got the impression of large wings and a compact body. Once again, it looked to be as big as one of those compact cars that gets great gas mileage.

Big Louie never knew what got him, I truly believe that, or I make myself believe that. There was a blood curdling scream from the man and then it grew higher in pitch until it abruptly ceased, like a light switch had been flicked. Ted and I were able to follow what happened next thanks to the flashlight, glowing in the dark.

One moment the flashlight was bobbing about four feet off the ground, and then it was airborne, moving high into the air like it had grown wings and taken flight. The light went about as high as the store roof and then the light stopped and began to plummet back to the earth. When it hit the ground, the bulb shattered and the area outside was cast once again into perpetual darkness.

Through the glass, I could have sworn I heard the sound of giant wings, but I still don't know if I imagined it or not.

I could hear Kyle crying, calling out for me and his mother and I turned away from the glass doors and moved back into the store, towards my son. Upon reaching him, I picked him up; nodding to Michelle that whatever had just happened was now over.

Ted walked back to Fred and the others and shook his head. "He's gone. Something took him, something big." His words laid heavy in the air as they all took in what they'd just heard. I believe most of them were still in shock. We were all average people and had never witnessed a gun battle from a few feet away.

Norman was still behind the counter, and suddenly he slumped forward, his head striking the top of the counter as he fell to the floor. There were cries of panic and Fred and Reuben went to the wounded man, picking him up and dragging him around the counter to the open floor. Buddy hovered around them, his face filled with concern for his old friend.

Gently, they laid him down and Bob moved the oil lantern closer to the old man's face. Norman's eyes were closed and it didn't look like he was breathing. Fred knelt down next to him and checked for a pulse. After a full minute had gone by, he took his hand away and shook his head.

"I think he's dead," he said softly.

"What? No way, get out of the way," Reuben ordered him and

checked, as well. After checking for a pulse and finding none, he searched the wound on Norman's shoulder and when he lifted Norman's arm, he saw there was blood on the inside of his armpit. Pulling a small pocket knife, Reuben cut the area free of material and then sighed heavily.

"Dammit, Norman, why couldn't you just give them some damn candy?"

"What, what is it?" Bob asked, kneeling down next to him.

Reuben lowered Norman's arm and placed the hand on the old man's chest, then did the same for the other one.

"The bullet went through his arm and into his side. I don't know for sure, but it could have hit anything from his lungs to his heart. If I had to guess though, I'd say he bled out internally." He shook his head again, gazing down at his friend. "Damn fool, well, at least you went out with a bang, and not in a hospital bed, you old war bird." Reuben looked up at Fred, Buddy and Ted. "He didn't want that," he said in a far away voice, "to wither away and die in a VA hospital somewhere. At least he had a warrior's death." He looked back down at Norman and brushed the dead man's white hair off his forehead. There was a dark blue and black bruise on the corner of his brow where he'd struck the counter when he had collapsed. "He was in W.W. 2, you know. We both were...Buddy, too."

"Yup, that's right; we were some of the last one's in Revere, too. Everyone's dying off lately," Buddy said as he gazed down at Norman's face.

No one answered, grieving for the dead man.

I stayed where I was and watched the tableau play out in front of me. Bob went to check on the three dead gangbangers, shaking his head upon returning to us when he was finished inspecting the last one.

Carl came out of the shadows and moved next to Fred. He whispered something into his ear and Fred frowned deeply.

"Oh, sweet Jesus, I'm afraid we have one more casualty from Norman's shootout," Fred said in a sad voice and moved into the aisles with Carl in the lead.

I perked up at that, looking around and counting who was missing in the flickering shadows. Then I realized Jordan was nowhere to be seen. Handing Kyle back to Michelle, my son not protesting in the least, as he was in a slight state of shock again after all the gunshots and screaming, I stood up.

My eyes went to the plate-glass windows lining the front of the store and I saw dozens of small shadows moving across the glass. At the time I didn't know they had been attracted to the hardware store from all the gunshots, the sounds echoing into the outer darkness beyond the building's walls. I turned away. There was really nothing I or any of us could do but pray none of those creatures had the idea to try and break the glass.

I needed to check on Jordan for myself. Jordan was a good man and I liked him, especially after he had made that toy for Kyle. Even as I moved towards Carl and Fred, the darker shape of Jordan lying immobile near their feet, I prayed they were mistaken.

If only I had known at the time that the stray bullet from Slim's gun--fired when he had been shot and killed--had managed to strike one of the upper plate-glass windows, leaving a small hole and a slight crack that would grow in time.

But that was a problem for another time; right now all I knew was that it was time to bury another one of us.

14

MORE TO BURY

TALK OF LEAVING

I STARED DOWN at Jordan's disfigured face and I had to look away.

There was no question the man was dead. Fred had a small flashlight in his hand, and as he played the beam over Jordan's face, I could see the jagged wound where the man's left eye had been.

Near him, on a shelf, two feet off the floor, there was a roll of pink insulation next to a half dozen more. There were a couple of small holes going completely through the entire roll of one of them, and it wasn't that hard to figure out what had happened.

When gunfire rang out, Jordan had dropped to the floor like the rest of us. But he had the bad luck of hiding behind nothing more solid than insulation and he was also almost right behind where Grille had stood, only an aisle over and slightly to the right. He had caught some stray buckshot from Norman's shotgun and the shrapnel had killed him when the searing lead had penetrated his brain through his eye socket. He probably never knew what hit him, if that was any consolation. I didn't think it was.

His other eye was still open and I reached out and closed it, sighing heavily.

"Christ, Fred, we're dropping like flies around here. We haven't been here for more than a day." I stood up, shaking my head as I placed my hands on my hips.

"Look, I want to tell you something I've been thinking about. I wasn't really sure until right now, but I think it's our only chance of staying alive."

Fred looked on with anticipation. "Yeah, so what is it? What's your great idea? Spill it."

I decided there was no going back now. So I just blurted it out.

"We need to get out of here and as soon as possible. Now, wait, don't say anything; hear me out. When that fat guy left the store, he got as far as your jeep before anything happened to him. I've been thinking about how those things out there hunt, and if I had to guess, I'd say it's one of two things. Sound, smell or both. In the dark they can't see anything anyway and have you noticed they don't seem to have any eyes?"

Fred nodded slowly, his brow creasing. "Come to think of it, yes, you're right."

"Maybe I am. Now, we can't do much about our smell, but if we can make enough noise, cause a distraction outside, I think we can make it to your jeep."

"So what? Okay, smart guy, so we get to Fred's jeep. What then?" Carl asked unctuously. "There's nowhere to go. We should wait here until help arrives. Surely the police or military will be here soon enough."

"But that's just it; we don't know if help is ever gonna arrive, Carl. I think we're on our own out here," I said.

"So I'll ask you again, where the hell do we go if we leave here?" Carl asked.

"Simple, we run for it, that's what. Pick a direction and just go. It's all we got. Or we stay here and wait to either starve or get eaten by those things, because Carl, sooner or later they are going to get in here again. But wherever we decide to go, first we need to swing by my house so I can get my wife. Fred can do the same for Margie, then Bob and Ted can go to their homes. Then we can go to your house, too, Carl, though if you think your wife is riding with us, you can forget it, there's not enough room."

Carl ground his teeth and his fists clenched tightly. His neck muscles grew taut and I swear to God I thought he was going to hit me.

"Go ahead, if you think you got the stones," I said in a low voice. We both stared at each other, neither wanting to be the one to break eye contact first. Normally, I would never be so aggressive, but I had a feeling it was all the stress. I'm sure it was getting to all of us.

"All right, you two, that's enough of that. I don't care who's got the bigger dick. Right now we need to work together," Fred said and then lowered his voice in a respectful way. "'Sides, we got more bodies to deal with."

That woke me up and I looked away from Carl, but made sure to keep the corner of my eye on him.

"Sorry, Fred, I don't know what I was thinkin'" I turned back to Carl. "Sorry, Carl, that was a cheap shot, I didn't mean it. I guess I'm just on edge."

Carl didn't reply, but instead pushed by me and moved back to the front of the hardware store. I stood there for almost ten seconds after he had gone, then muttered a low: "Asshole."

"Now, John, don't be like that. I'm sure his wife is a touchy subject with him. 'Sides, those things probably already got to her. Let's face it, John; she couldn't move that fast and those beasties are mighty quick. And I'm sure Carl knows that deep in his heart."

"Yeah, guess you're right, too bad, I do feel sorry for the guy, I guess, a little anyway."

Fred smiled slightly in the light of his flashlight. He gestured with the light beam to Jordan lying patiently below us on the floor.

"Shall we get the dolly and lay this poor soul to rest?"

"Yeah, guess we should, huh? Then we got to get those other assholes that caused all this shit in the first place."

I went to get the dolly and was back in minutes. Fred was still standing over Jordan, waiting for me. In the shadows of the aisle I could see he was deep in thought and when he heard the dolly, he looked up.

"You all right?" I asked him.

"Yes, John, I'm fine. I was just thinking a little."

I slowed when I reached Jordan and then leaned down and grabbed the body under the arms, cringing slightly that I was touching another dead body, but I fought the willies off.

Fred took the legs of the body and lifted carefully, not wanting to hurt himself. Actually, I did most of the work. I didn't mind.

Our conversation never stopped as we lifted Jordan's corpse onto the dolly.

"So what were you thinking about?" I asked after I set Jordan's body gently onto the dolly.

"Oh, not that much, I just had a little bit of a premonition."

"About what?" I asked. God, he was being cryptic, more so than usual.

"That these poor souls who are no longer with us might just be the lucky ones amongst us."

I didn't answer him, I didn't want to. What he said was too close to what I had been feeling, but didn't want to admit to myself. For my son's sake if for no other reason.

In silence, we wheeled the dolly to the back room so Jordan could join Shaun, his one true love, even if he had to wait until death to do so.

15

PLANS TO LEAVE

AFTER THE THREE gangbangers were brought to the back room and dumped unceremoniously into a new pile, we all gathered around the counter at the front of the store where Norman had held his audience like a great king. I took one thought with me from the back room, which was, it was really getting crowded back there.

Michelle stood next to me and I was very conscious of her soft body touching me through my clothes. I began getting aroused and I forced it down, thinking about death, baseball and Carl's wife. That last one did it and I found myself calming down.

Kyle was sitting on the counter between me and Michelle and I had my arm around him. He was swinging his feet back and forth and I don't believe he even knew he was doing it. He was munching happily on a chocolate bar and once again I was amazed at the resiliency of youth. Or better yet, how he was able to compartmentalize what was happening to him. He knew we were in mortal danger, even at his young age, but yet he had the high spirits to swing his legs as if he hadn't a care in the world.

Also, I had a new item in the back pocket of my pants. I now carried a gun. It was the one Slim had used to kill Norman with.

When I had returned to the counter; coming from the back room after disposing of the bodies, Ted had walked over with it in is hand and had handed it to me with a slight grin.

"Here, John, some of us were talking and we thought you should hold this."

"Me? Why?" I asked. I was totally clueless why of all the people in the hardware store; I should be the holder of the fabled ring, so to speak.

Ted merely shrugged and looked away, not wanting to keep eye contact with me.

"Well, we just thought, uhm, you know, because of Kyle. Uhm, if things get bad and you have to... I mean, if it's a no choice situation..."

I saved him from continuing by placing my hand on his shoulder.

"No, it's okay, Ted, I get it. And thank you; tell the others, too, or better yet, I will when I talk to them."

Ted only nodded and walked away, his shoulders slumped. I watched him go and realized I had a totally different view of this man who I had disliked so much because he didn't keep his grass maintained. Now, those things seemed so ridiculous that I felt ashamed I had ever brought them up in the first place. I knew if we lived through whatever was happening to us all, we would become steadfast friends for a very long time to come.

Fred was talking to us all and had some drawings to show us, as well.

"Ever since John spoke to me a little while ago I've been thinking about what he said and I think he's right. So I came up with an idea that should get us to my jeep safe and sound. If anyone has their own car out there near mine, they are more than welcome to go to it, too."

He pointed to the first drawing, more of a diagram actually, and began rattling off the different points of interest.

"Okay, first we build a box with some of that old plywood in the back room near the boiler and we make it so it can fit all of us. There are cordless tools that should do the job easily and we've got a lot of extra rechargeable batteries in boxes in the back room. Usually they have some kind of a charge when you open them, even though the instructions say they don't. Plus, we can always use hand tools, not that most of you even know what that's like. In my time, we actually used a hammer to put a nail into a piece of wood."

Buddy and Reuben both nodded, the old folks gang still going strong.

"Second, we make a door on the front of the box so when we get to the jeep, all we have to do is open the door and climb in." He pointed to some poles on each end of the box. "These are mops. The tops of the mops can get soaked in lighter fluid and then we light them before we go outside. That should give us some much needed light and should keep anything from climbing on top of us. We can also use some one pound propane tanks with attachments on them, which should work well to protect our feet and legs." He then moved to the sides where there were small flaps in the wood, like mail slots on a house door, only larger. "These are so once we're out there we can toss power tools away from us that make noise. If John is right, then the bastards should investigate, thereby giving us the time to get into the jeep safely." He pointed to the bottom of the box. "This is the only flaw in my design. The bottom has to be open so we can move quickly. So our feet will be vulnerable. I can't figure out how to get around this, so if anyone has an idea while we're building it then speak up. At least we can use the propane torches to keep them away, I hope. All right then, that's it, I'm done. If all goes as planned, it should only take an hour or two at most to build this to my general specifications. It doesn't have to be exact, this is just an idea."

He looked at each of our faces, waiting for any questions. "Well, what do you think?"

Bob nodded, rubbing his chin, and Ted grinned widely. Both Buddy and Reuben were muttering to themselves, but it was in the positive. Earl didn't seem to care one way or the other and Carl wasn't really paying attention.

This was even better than I had hoped. Fred had invented a small, mobile tank for people to move about in. I slapped my hands on the table, pleased with Fred's idea to no end. I glanced at everyone one at a time and smiled widely and asked: "So, when do we get started?"

16

CONSTRUCTION

THE WORK WAS hot and sweaty.

With no air circulating in the hardware store, it wasn't long before we were all hot and sticky. The bodies in the back room had already begun to smell and Buddy took the initiative and used the dolly to grab all the bags of potting soil from the store shelves and pour them on top of the corpses. That helped to dull the flies already appearing and I had to wonder where the hell they had come from.

The potting soil helped a little and made it easier to take our minds off our fallen friends.

Bob, Ted and I did most of the work cutting and securing the wood together. Ted was invaluable with this. He was skilled with the use of both saw and hammer, and so had taken the job of foreman. Fred hovered nearby; pointing out mistakes we might have been making and giving us his opinion on how we could fix them.

Kyle helped, too. I gave him a small hammer and a box of nails and let him go to town on a couple of broomsticks. I instructed him to place the nails all over the end of the wood, thereby making a crude weapon. He didn't do a very good job, but that was okay. Really, I just wanted him to stay busy, as we all did, by working. With something to concentrate on, a real problem to solve, it was easier to take our minds off our dire situation.

The real question was not why didn't we all go mad, but why any of us were able to remain sane under such overwhelming obstacles.

Reuben sat on his old stool at the counter, honing points on a few of the remaining broomsticks. He even took a few handles off some rakes and shovels we didn't need and made spears out of them. Earl, who I believe was the oldest of the geriatric bunch, just kept Reuben company.

Buddy was our extra man, helping wherever he was needed. Buddy was the one that gathered all the charcoal lighter fluid and Bic lighters and set them near the front of the store. Carl did very little and I decided from the beginning of the project to keep it that way. The man wasn't very handy, so would only get in the way.

Michelle helped with the cleanup, sweeping up the saw dust and woodchips and getting us tools when we needed them. She was also the mandatory battery changer. We went through more than twenty cordless batteries before we'd finished cutting the plywood and two-by-fours needed to make the box. We had about a dozen left over, which was more than enough for any extra cutting, and the few we would need to use for distractions when we tossed the power tools away from us as we made our way to Fred's jeep.

I felt my stomach growing uneasy, clenching into knots, the closer we came to finishing.

We had all decided to rest after finishing the box, and after we had some sleep, we would pack up whatever water and food we could scrape together and take our chances on the road.

There were now more of those scorpion creatures on the front windows of the store, too, and I guessed they might have been everywhere, covering the roof and stone walls that made up the rest of the building. But all they did is move around, and though unsettling, wasn't threatening. I suspected they were being attracted to all our sawing and hammering. I'm sure the noise we were making was quite loud, despite the fact we were in the middle of the store. We had taken out a few shelving units so we had more room to work and the miscellaneous items were piled in a far corner. I'm sure if Norman had still been with us, he would have been quite upset at the condition of his life's work. The hardware store was now a complete shambles, with items askew and some lying broken and shattered on the ground. The small section that had held lamps were nothing but broken vases and crushed light shades.

A few times while I was working on the wooden box, I glanced out the front windows and saw those large bat shapes come right up to the plate-glass. There would be a darker shape which would hover in the air for a half-second and then it would be gone as fast as it was there. When it retreated, there would be one less of the scorpion creatures clinging to the plate-glass.

It was a regular jungle out there in the darkness, where each creature fed on the other, and now humans were part of that food chain.

A little less than two hours later, with all of us exhausted, we were finished.

Fred nodded in approval, inspecting the flaps on the sides of the small wooden tank and the door that would be the front. From the inside out, we had sunk nails through almost the entire box, the points coming out to make the entire cube look like a square porcupine. That was Bob's idea and hadn't been in the initial plans. He hoped that would keep the beasts from crawling onto the box or trying to cut into it with their pincers. Mop handles were attached on all sides and three in the middle, held on with steel shelf brackets. The mop handles had been cut so only a foot jutted up from the roof and made the cube look like some kind of Medieval Trojan horse. I tried to imagine the mop heads on fire, burning like torches.

Reuben came over and dropped an armful of broomsticks on the floor, the pile rattling when they landed. Each tip had been whittled to a sharp point. Inside the box, on both walls, curved hooks had been attached and the spears would go into them so that they would be ready when needed.

I took a step back and inspected our creation. All this to simply walk a few car lengths. But I knew we would be fighting for every step we took.

Small sounds of scratching from the front of the store caused all of us to look at the plate-glass again.

"There's more of them arriving every second," Ted said while he moved his eyes back and forth, trying to follow each dark shape.

"Where the hell are they all coming from?" Bob asked while taking a step forward to get a better look.

No one could answer him, because there was no real answer to give. Whatever had happened to the sun, causing the world to descend into darkness, was the stuff of fairy tales and fantasy. Everything we knew and believed; the laws of physics and what was reality, had been tossed away like an empty beer can. The world we knew was gone and none of us had any idea if it would ever return. So we now had two choices. Except the world the way it was, or die, like so many others before us.

I chose to deal with my new environment and survive; if not for me, than for my son.

"Let's get this thing near the front doors so it'll be ready to go when we are," Fred suggested, trying to get us to focus on the task at hand. It worked and I pulled my eyes away from the scuttling shapes on the glass and moved to the rear of the wooden cube. Ted and Bob did the same, and while being careful of the protruding nails, we picked up the box and carried it to the double doors that would lead to the outer world. Fred had a tape measure and double checked one more time that it would fit through the frame when both doors were opened. He smiled when he finished, satisfied, that yes, it would fit.

"Wouldn't it have been hilarious if we had made it too big?" He asked as he tucked the tape measure into one of his pockets.

"No," I said, not amused in the slightest, "it would not have been funny."

Fred merely shrugged at my disagreement and moved away to confer with Reuben.

Fred talked to Reuben for less than a minute and then turned to the rest of us, a smile creasing his lips. Kyle was standing near my legs and Michelle was on my right. Without thinking, I wrapped my arm around her. She smiled and leaned in closer.

"Okay, people, great job. The box is finished. Normally, I'd say we should wait until sunup to head out, but as that's not gonna happen…" He got a few slight chuckles, but it was morbid humor and no one was really in the mood. So, I suggest we all get some rest and after we've had a few hours of shuteye, we go for it and make a run for my jeep. Anyone object?"

No one did, and after a few pats on the back to each other for a job well done, we all went our separate ways, pairing up into groups again and bedding down. I found it rather amusing to watch as different people went with each other. With Michelle by my side, and of course, Kyle, too, the three of us went to one of the untouched aisles against the north-side wall and sank to the floor with tired limbs. Norman had a display of small throw rugs on one of the shelves and I took a few off the bottom shelf and spread them on the floor, which Michelle thanked me immensely for doing. There were a lot of rugs, actually, so I gave the rest out to the others, who thanked me. As I began passing out the rugs, I was able to see who was sitting where in the store.

Buddy, Reuben, Earl and Fred joined up and sat down at the counter again, a deck of cards magically appearing while the men chatted for a little while before bedding down themselves. I noticed a bottle of whiskey in between them on the counter and guessed it must have been Norman's.

Fred saw me looking and held up the bottle for me to see. I shook my head no and he nodded. Whiskey wouldn't do me much good, all it would probably do is make me sick or tired, or both. I'd never been much of a drinker and didn't feel the need to dull my senses anymore than they already were.

Bob and Ted were together, and I saw Carl was with them, as well. Bob had always had a soft spot for Carl, though I had no idea why. Before I headed back to my little campsite, I made sure to grab two sodas and a couple of candy bars from off the counter. Though it was terrible so many of us were dead, at least with the loss of so many people we now had more food to go around.

With food now in hand, I went back to Michelle and Kyle, looking forward to a few hours of sleep.

More sounds of scratching behind me caused me to look over my shoulder at the plate-glass windows. There were now even more of those creatures on the plate-glass and I had a feeling if there was light outside, it would be almost entirely blocked by the bodies crawling across the glass. Every oil lantern in the hardware store was lit, plus as many candles as we could find. It made constructing the box easier and no one felt the need to extinguish them. I preferred the light, and in some small way felt safer with all the oil lanterns and candles keeping the shadows at bay. The flashlights had been packed neatly inside an old, dusty and worn backpack that had been sitting behind the counter in a cardboard box labeled: lost and found. There had been other miscellaneous items in the cardboard box, as well. One lone mitten, left over from the passing winter, a set of car keys with a keychain on it that said: I love my cat. A couple of T passes that were more than a year old and one baseball cap with the symbol for the New York Yankees. I didn't believe anyone would ever try to claim that, not in this city. We were all loyal Red Sox fans and were proud of it.

The dusty backpack was lying next to a few bags of the remaining candy and soda cans, ready to go in what I guess we would soon call the morning, though in name only.

I felt a shiver go down my back and I tried to shake it off.

But no matter how hard I tried, the feeling of dread that had insinuated itself inside me would not go away.

I told myself this feeling of dread which had come over me was just nerves, and it was no worse than what I had already been feeling.

So I ignored it.

Looking back at the decision I made at the time, I truly believe even if I had known what was to come, I doubt I would have been able to stop it, no matter how much I might have wanted to.

17

OVERRUN

A DASH FOR FREEDOM

I WAS THE first one to wake up. Though at the time, I didn't know this.

My bladder was my silent alarm clock and the soda and water I had drunk a few hours ago was ready to leave my body.

Scratching my head, I looked around at the dim gloom surrounding me. Michelle was curled up in a ball with Kyle and I gazed down at them both. Michelle's hair had spread out around her like a golden halo, and even in the wan light of the oil lanterns, she looked like an angel. I was falling in love with her all over again and I wasn't relishing bringing her back to my home. It would be more than a little awkward with both she and Karen together in the same house, but I'd decided after we first made love that I would deal with that later.

The first item on the agenda would be to make it to my house.

Climbing to my feet, I stretched and was about to head to the bathroom, not relishing the darkness that awaited me, when I heard a very soft sound of something breaking, like broken crystal falling onto carpeting. At first, my mind wandered as I tried to decipher the sound I'd heard through the fog of sleep. Then it came again, slightly louder, though I'd have to say this time it sounded more like an egg being cracked.

Forgetting about my bladder, I moved to the front of the hardware store, my ears straining to piece together the sounds I was hearing. I picked up one of the oil lanterns from off the counter, clearing the shadows away like a sharp wind to fog.

Wait!

There it was again, louder than before now that I was closer.

I held the oil lantern up by my head, with my arm stretched out like one of those ceramic jockeys you see on people's lawns in the spring and summer. Slowly, I played the light of the oil lantern over the plate-glass windows, searching for that subtle sound of cracking eggs.

Then I heard it again and I looked up to the top of the glass; right where the ceiling met the top frames of metal. The light of the oil lantern could barely pierce the darkness far overhead by the ceiling, but I just managed to make out what was making that damn sound.

And as I looked on the cracking glass, my blood turned to ice water in my veins and my heart froze in my chest. Even as I watched, the first scorpion-creature was wiggling through the hole where Slim's bullet had pierced the plate-glass. It wiggled like a worm, small pieces of the glass falling away while it worked its pincers at the edges of the slowly growing hole.

I wondered for how many hours that thing had been up there, working at the hole until it finally had enough room to try and squeeze through. I didn't even think about what might have happened if I hadn't woken up.

I assume we would have had a repeat of the day before, only this time; it would have been too late for us all.

Without hesitation, my mouth already opening, I spun around and yelled at the top of my voice, almost shrieking in my fear and terror of what I knew was coming.

"They're in! They're inside with us! Get the hell up. Get up, now!"

While I was yelling my warning, I was charging back to Michelle and Kyle. My stocking feet slid along the linoleum and I almost fell on top of Michelle who was staring around in a daze, not understanding what was happening,

"What?" She said in a slur. Drool was on the corner of her mouth and the side of her face had indentations from the rug pressed into her skin, like wrinkles.

I shook Kyle hard, probably much harder than I should have. He turned over and his eyes were open, but I think he was still sleeping. My son had a way of doing that. Sometimes in the middle of the night, I would go into his room and pick up any toys on the floor near his bed, that way, if he needed to go to the bathroom in the middle of the night, he wouldn't trip on the toys while he made his way to the bathroom. Sometimes he would wake up as I entered and his eyes would be open, but it was like he was seeing someplace else and didn't even know I was in the room. He had this look now.

Trying to calm down, knowing panic would doom both myself and the rest of us, I gently picked Kyle up.

"Come on, son, we have to get up." I didn't have the heart to tell him why, knowing it would terrify him.

Michelle was awake now, and so were the others. All around me, I could hear yelling as everyone gathered their clothing and prepared to fight the creatures off once again. A small thought went through my mind like a spark. I wondered who we would lose this time.

"Michelle, watch Kyle," I said. "Here, take this," I shoved the small gun into her hand, wanting her to have it to protect Kyle.

"But I..."

I cut her off; there was no time for debates right now.

"Later," I said, and thought to myself, if there was a later.

Thrusting my feet into my sneakers, I ignored the laces, knowing time was of the essence. Bob ran past my aisle and I saw he had the same shovel he'd used before. Hopefully, he would have as much luck with it as the last time. I glanced forward to the front windows and my jaw fell open when I saw the creatures pouring in. One at a time, but never ceasing, they just kept coming. They swarmed over the ceiling, clinging like spiders, and I made a quick guess there was at least forty or fifty; and they were still coming.

It took me only a fraction of a second to realize we wouldn't be able to fight off this many, not without sustaining serious casualties.

"Come on, come with me!" I yelled to Michelle, and she did what she was told, Kyle in her arms. Kyle was still quiet, not quite understanding what was happening, his eyes darting around like he was drunk.

As we ran down the aisle, I grabbed the first thing I saw that could be used as a weapon; a solid metal curtain rod from the drapery section.

Reaching the counter, I was joined by Fred and Ted.

"Sweet Jesus, what the hell is going on here? How did they get inside the store?" Fred asked this while the entire time his eyes were darting back and forth as he searched the shadows surrounding him in terror. He was holding a garden hoe and I sure hoped he knew how to use it.

"That doesn't matter now, what matters is there's too many of them. Fred, we need to go right now! We need to get to your car right fucking now!" I almost screamed the last words, but held back, not wanting to scare Kyle.

"What? Now? But the plan?"

"Screw the plan," I snapped at him. "We've got about five seconds before they're everywhere!" As if to prove my point, five of the scorpions dropped down from the ceiling, mouths snapping and pincers clicking.

Ted had a pitchfork for a weapon, and with me and Fred by his side, we attacked the creatures, whacking them and puncturing their hard-shelled bodies. But no sooner did we finish them off when a dozen more fell from the ceiling behind us.

Nearby us, someone ran by and in their panic struck an oil lantern. It fell to the floor and burst, the oil igniting, flames rising as it began seeking more fuel.

No sooner did that fire begin then three creatures fell from the ceiling and landed on a couple more oil lanterns on the counter, knocking the fixtures to the floor as the creatures struggled to right themselves and go on the attack. The lantern bases shattered when they struck the floor, oil splashing across the tiles like water, but not igniting. A moment later, a stray candle fell from its holder and the oil became liquid fire.

The flames shot up, lighting the store in its brilliance and burning more than two dozen creatures. Their squeals of pain filled the store and I almost dropped my weapon in shear pain when the sound penetrated my ear drums. It was like a hundred fingernails on a hundred chalkboards.

I heard someone yell in fear from across the store and I turned to see Reuben, Buddy, Earl and Carl being herded into a corner like sheep by more than a dozen of the creatures. In the shadows and chaos, I don't think any of the four men realized they were committing suicide by not fighting back and breaking through the creature's ranks and back into the open.

Buddy had a knife in his hand and he stabbed at one of the creatures as it climbed onto the shelf near his head. He sliced at it and cut off three of its legs. Yellow blood shot out and caught Earl on the left arm as the man hovered behind Buddy. The old man screamed in pain as the blood ate away his arm, flesh first and then the bone. While I watched in horror, the man's limb simply fell off, leaving a jagged, acid wound that was at least cauterized. It was still possible the old man could live beyond his injury if he would only escape and run for the box. Reuben went to Earl, supporting the man from falling over from shock and pain.

They were fighting off more than two dozen of the creatures by now and Bob was on the edge of the things, trying to clear a path to the trapped men. He was flattening the scorpions like he was a machine, yellow ichor flying everywhere with each blow of the shovel. His muscles shone with sweat as he worked the shovel, resembling a railroad worker nailing spikes into timbers, but no matter how many he killed, there were just too many. I could only watch in horror as the four men were overrun by the creatures, pincers slicing into their legs and feet to make the men unstable and fall to the floor, their sliced ankles and calves no longer able to support them. The last thing I saw before the four men were covered in the gray carapaces of the scorpions was Buddy grabbing two, one pound propane tanks from off the shelf behind him and breaking the seals on the ends. I glimpsed his face for just a second and saw no fear there, only a grim resolve to go down fighting.

A warrior's death, I thought, just like Norman.

With the seal on the tanks broken, the flammable gas escaping into the air, Buddy pulled a Bic lighter from his pocket, and without hesitation, flicked the wheel.

"See you in Hell, you bastards!" He screamed as he flicked the wheel.

A small explosion blossomed for an instant when the small tanks of flammable gas ignited, swallowing the men whole. The smell of charred and roasting meat came to my nose, and when the flames died down, there was only charcoaled corpses and burnt carapaces of the creatures littering the area.

"Oh my God!" Fred screamed as he watched the fireball dissipate. But there was no time to mourn. The fires from the shattered oil lanterns were spreading, the flames following the items on the shelves and continuing onward like a river.

Paint cans began exploding when their contents boiled from within from the intense heat and plastic one gallon jugs of paint thinner melted, leaking out, the thinner then adding to the fire.

The caustic smoke was becoming unbearable and I grabbed Fred by the arm and shoved him forward toward our wooden box, dragging Michelle along behind me. We were quickly running out of time and staying to fight was out of the question. The flames were growing hotter, and if we stayed for much longer, we would all die of smoke inhalation and then burn in the flames.

Twenty creatures blocked our path and I charged them with the metal curtain rod, swinging the tip back and forth a foot off the ground. Fred was whacking overhand at the creatures, the end of the hoe sinking deeply into legs and carapaces. Ted arrived on my right and he was doing his own share of damage. If there weren't so many, we could have probably taken them, but there were now what seemed like hundreds inside the hardware store and more were coming in with each passing second.

Bob was sitting on the floor a few feet from me, shaking his head as he tried to clear it. He'd been thrown from the propane tanks exploding and was only now picking himself up. His face was beet red from the heat of the blast and he had pockmarks on his face and shirt from where the yellow blood had splattered him.

"Bob, get to the box, it's our only chance!" I yelled. Behind me, I heard explosions as flammables combusted from the heat of the inferno. I could feel the flames on my back and knew there would be no retreating.

I checked over my shoulder to make sure Michelle and Kyle were still with me. A half dozen creatures came from behind her and I spun around, kicking two away at the risk of losing a foot and swiping the other four with the curtain rod like I was playing croquet. I didn't care if I killed them; I was just trying to stall for time.

Fred and Ted moved across the floor, making their way slowly towards the box. Above our heads, only six feet away, a large piece of plate-glass fell in, the creatures now pouring in like water from a breached dam. We had only seconds or we were all dead.

Spinning around after getting rid of the attacking creatures, I ran forward, toward the box. Kyle was screaming now at the top of his lungs, the kind of scream that says: I'm so scared I can't stand it. I never agreed with him more than right now.

Bob was on his feet again and back in action. He was squishing the scorpions like giant flies. The metal of the shovel was pitting to the point it would soon start to have holes in it. The blood of those things was strong enough to eat through metal and I cringed inside thinking about what it would feel like on my skin. Then I didn't have to wonder when Ted nailed one near me and its yellow blood splashed on my arm. I yelped in pain and my skin sizzled, but then it stopped. I was lucky; the droplets had been very small.

We moved across the floor, covering the remaining distance, and it was a battle every second of the way. Michelle, with Kyle in her arms, was in the middle of us and the rest of us were surrounding her like she was our queen.

Whack, crunch, kick, repeat; we struck again and again, leaving a pile of small bodies in our wake.

When we reached the wooden box, Bob managed to get it open, and I literally kicked Michelle and Kyle inside, breathing a small sigh of relief when they at least were safe, though not by much.

Behind us, the store was a raging inferno, the flames reaching to the ceiling. The air was so caustic I could barely see and my throat burned from the fumes.

"Get inside the box, we need to go!" I yelled to Fred and Ted. They did as they were told, making a sweep with their weapons and then diving inside. Ted reached over and grabbed the packs of food and water and then hung them inside on one of the hooks we made for just that reason.

Now it was only Bob and I still in the store, and I backed up until I was poked by one of the nails jutting from the outside of the box.

"Bob, light the mops, I'll watch your back!"

Nodding, Bob smashed three more of the creatures to pulp and then spun around, picking up two cans of lighter fluid and spraying them onto the mop heads. He was rushing and a lot of fluid spilled onto the top of the box, but it couldn't be helped. Dropping the empty cans, he pulled a Bic lighter out of his pocket--we all had one, as we had divided them amongst ourselves earlier—and lit the first mop head.

The torch sprang to life, the fire burning brightly and he quickly lit two others. The rest were ignored, there was no time.

The box was five feet from the double-glass doors and the creatures were covering the floor like a living carpet.

"Come on, get inside!" I yelled. "You've done enough!"

He turned, kicked three more aside and dived for the door, opening it, and falling in a heap of limbs inside the box. I was right behind him, and after falling in, as well, Fred catching me, thankfully, the door was slammed shut behind me.

Inside the box we were now safe for a few precious seconds and we all were breathing heavily, trying to calm down.

It was stuffy inside the small cube and our breathing was labored, but at least the smoke wasn't as bad.

"Godammit, what the hell happened to Carl and the others?" Ted yelled as he looked around in the darkness of the cube.

I quickly filled Ted in and the man cursed again, his hand punching the wall in anger.

"Okay, let's get going, the fires getting worse," Fred said as he moved to the front of the cube. "There's no time to mourn for them now. We need to go before we burn up."

Michelle was in the back and Kyle was with her, though in the semi-darkness, I couldn't see them very well. The fire outside was so bright, light actually penetrated slightly through any small cracks and seams where we had connected the pieces of wood.

"On three we all need to lift," Fred said and began counting.

And on three we all pushed up on the ceiling, our heads and hands doing the work. The box rose a few inches off the ground and we began walking, or more like shuffling. We pushed the scorpions out of the way as we went, and the creatures snapped at the strange box that was now protecting their prey from them. We were like a snow plow, plowing the things to the side and in front of us. They were knocked over and rolled along while we pushed our way to the double doors.

But when we reached the doors, we were still trapped.

"Oh shit, you've got to be kidding me!" Bob yelled as he pushed forward on the box, but it didn't move. "The damn doors are still locked. There's no way we can get by them."

"What are you saying?" I asked hesitantly.

Bob's face was grim. "One of us has to go out there again and unlock the doors and chalk them open."

"But that's suicide. They're everywhere by now. Shit, even when someone tries to leave, they're gonna try to get inside here with us." That came from Ted.

"Hey, if you got any better ideas, I'm all ears," Bob quipped back.

But no one did. This hadn't been part of the plan. We weren't supposed to be overrun while we tried to run for the jeep.

"So who goes?" Fred asked, looking at each of us in the darkness. He couldn't see our faces, so had no way of knowing our reactions to his question.

At first, no one answered. There were only three choices anyway. I know neither Fred nor Ted would make Michelle go, not with Kyle quivering in her arms, so it had to be one of us.

We were running out of time and I knew if someone didn't go out there we would all die, so the choice was easy for me.

"I'll go," I said flatly. I wasn't even scared; my only thoughts being for my son. "You guys just make damn sure you get out of here in one piece. I don't want to die for nothing." Then I pushed my way to the front of the box. "I love you, Kyle," I said as I began reaching for the door latch.

Just before my hand found the small latch that held the door closed, I felt something brush my head and I was grabbed from behind.

"Forget it, John, If anyone's gonna be a hero, it's gonna be me. You got a son to think about. Just make sure you check on my wife when you get back home. Tell her I love her." And before I could protest, Bob pushed by me and was charging back into the hardware store. Acting fast, I kicked three of the creatures away from me when they tried to get inside the box, but the door opening pushed almost all of them away, saving us from being overrun. I grabbed the door and slammed it closed, more small bodies bouncing off the wood as we all coughed from the smoke filling the building.

I opened the side flap on the right side of the box and was able to see everything Bob did next.

Upon leaving the safety of the box, Bob charged into the store and picked up his shovel lying on the floor behind him. A set of pincers nicked his hand and he cried out. Blood seeped down his knuckles, but he ignored it. He had a job to do, and dammit, he was going to do it, his hard visage told me so.

Whacking the things like he was playing golf, he moved to the glass doors. After clearing a path, he opened the lock and pushed the left door open. The door clicked when it was fully open and he returned for the next one. Six scorpions attacked him, nipping at his ankles and causing them to bleed. Limping, Bob kept going, knowing he was almost there. Reaching up, he unlocked the bolt that went into the top of the door frame and pushed the door open. This door didn't click when it was fully open and he cursed. It was broken and would have to be chalked or held open.

"Come on, you guys, move that fucking thing out of there!" He yelled while he held the second door open with his back. He knew if he didn't, the door would jam the box and it wouldn't fit. Only two inches on both sides was the clearance, because when we had built it, we had thought we were going to have four more people inside and would need the room for all the extra bodies.

But our numbers had been reduced drastically and now there were only four of us to move the heavy box. The ½ inch plywood was heavy and the tools, food and gear hanging from the walls inside only added to the weight.

With my hands pushing upwards on the ceiling, my head was also doing some of the lifting, the hard wood causing my scalp to protest the weight on it and I felt a kink in my neck.

But we managed to move forward, and though our footsteps were not in sync in the least, the box slid through the open doors. A thought came to me as we were shuffling our feet across the floor that we should have made the box with wheels on it, but at the time, no one had thought of it and it was a little late to be making alterations now.

We were off course and the left side was scraping the door handle, gouging into the wood and holding us up. Bob realized this and he used the shovel, wedging the scored tip through the doorframe and then pushing on the handle. The handle snapped in half, but not before we were catapulted free of the frame.

We were out of the store, we were free!

Well sort of.

Pushing by Michelle, I opened the rear flap to call to Bob, to get him to come back and get inside with us where it was safe, but Bob wasn't going to be joining us. I could only watch in horror as the tall, muscular man fought creature after creature, punching and kicking at them like a madman.

In the flickering firelight, I saw his face only once and his features were contorted into abject rage. Even if he could have heard me, I don't think my voice would have penetrated his mind. He was lost in a battle he could never win, but he was damn sure going to try.

One of the scorpions jumped onto the back of another one and then leaped for Bob's face. But the man was quicker and he grabbed it in mid-air with both his hands, holding the snapping pincers only inches from his face.

Then he squeezed his hands like a vice, and the front segment of the thing cracked and yellow ichor splattered everywhere. Bob's face was covered in acid and he dropped the half-dead squirming creature, his hands going to his face.

"Bob! Oh, Christ, no!" I screamed, wanting to go out there and save him, but knew it was hopeless,

Bob was screaming now, and when he turned my way, I could see his face was melted clean off! The flesh now resembled melted wax. His lips and eyes were gone and his nose slid from his face to fall to the ground where a creature picked it up and devoured it whole.

I couldn't even imagine the agony he must be in and my stomach flipped inside me as I continued to watch helplessly.

With Bob not able to defend himself, the scorpions attacked him in force, swarming over him, pincers sinking into his flesh again and again. Bob roared in anguish, turned around, and with faltering steps reentered the burning hardware store.

My jaw was hanging open as I watched him slowly move deeper into the store. His body was outlined against the flames and I could see more than a dozen things crawling all over him, more waiting for their chance. I couldn't believe he was still able to move, let alone walk, but after knowing the man better in the past day and a half, I had come to know he had a will of iron.

Pincers sliced at his ankle and he went down to one knee, but still he fought, grabbing creatures by their multiple legs and tossing them away. Another slice to the other leg and he was down to both knees, but still he continued forward. The inferno was only a few feet away and I imagined he could feel the heat on his face, or what was left of it.

More creatures covered him until it looked like he was wearing a living coat and then he finally reached the flames. I still don't know how he did it, but he managed to stand up again on his butchered legs one last time, despite the gashes in critical areas, and swayed like a drunkard for one critical moment. He was like the incarnation of the Devil made real, standing before his alter of flames with his minions crawling all over him.

"Bob," I said in a whisper, my eyes unable to look away.

Then Bob took one last step forward and tumbled into the flames, disappearing from view as the red and yellow inferno swallowed him whole. I don't know if it was my imagination, but I thought I heard the creatures' high-pitched squeals when Bob fell into the rolling fire, but it might have been my imagination. My blood was pounding so hard it sounded like jungle drums in my head.

"John, is he…?" Fred asked from behind me.

I nodded, but realizing he couldn't see me, I whispered. "Yeah, he is."

"Jesus Christ," Ted said, making the sign of the cross. "We're all gonna die. It's over, man, we can't fight this, its death itself. We're all dead and this is Hell. Yes, that's it, we're all dead and we've gone to Hell. That explains the darkness. He who is evil will spend eternity in darkness," he said this with his voice becoming hysterical.

Pincers were all over the wood of the box, the nails only helping a little, but for the present moment we appeared to be safe. Fred lit a lighter, casting all of our faces in a dull yellow glow. Looking at Ted, I saw his eyes were wide and sanity had left him.

Grabbing him by the shirt, I shook him back and forth, his head bouncing off the side wall, the flame of the lighter bouncing around as his body was jerked in rhythm to his body, and in the confines of the cube he kept bumping into Fred.

"Dammit, Ted, snap out of it. We're not gonna die; now stop talking that shit. My son is here and I don't want him to hear stuff like that. You got me?" While I yelled at him, I was still shaking him, and in the dim light of the cigarette lighter, Ted's face seemed to calm slightly. His eyes began to focus and then he was looking at me, not through me.

"Huh. What? Oh shit, John, I don't know what to say. Christ, I lost it there for a minute. I'm okay, now." He looked at Kyle who was in a state of shock and tried to smile at him.

Kyle's eyes were wide and his face was beet red. I wished I had time to hug him, but knew we needed to move. We were so vulnerable now it was too frightening to contemplate.

I glanced at Michelle and she smiled at me wanly. I could only imagine what she was feeling. Fear, terror, or outright horror was a few feelings that came to mind.

"Okay, Bob's gone and he gave his life so we could get out of here. Now let's not waste his sacrifice," I said. I looked at Fred's wrinkled visage, every wrinkle exposed from the flame of the lighter. "Fred, where's your jeep from here. We need to get there, now."

Fred turned around just as the lighter went out and opened the flap closest to him. He scanned the area, his eyes flicking back and forth as he searched the parking lot. The mop heads burned brightly above us, casting the parking lot in an ethereal glow. Shapes were moving out there, some too close to contemplate.

Fred yelled and his head snapped away from the flap. A pincer poked inside the rectangle hole, jumping up and down as it tried to get at us, and I used one of the power tools to drill at it. The drill sank deep and the pincer backed out of the hole.

"Shit, that was close," Fred gasped. "Almost lost an eye."

"Well, you didn't, so which way do we go?" I asked with impatience.

"That way," Fred pointed. "My jeep is about twenty-five feet or so that way."

"All right then, let's get moving," I told everyone.

With a heave, we pushed up on the box, and began shuffling our feet. I noticed for the first time the musty odor of sweat and body odor, some coming from me and some emanating from the others.

"Try to stay in the middle so they can't get at your feet," I said as I looked down to see pincers raking the ground under the few inches of space the box left as we lifted it. It was like there were men outside with blades and they were dragging them along the ground, trying to cut our feet out from under us. Michelle screamed when one nicked her sneaker, but only the rubber was sliced. She moved closer to me and we moved on.

We were halfway there when Fred cried out, falling to one knee. In the darkness of the box, I didn't realize he had fallen until I literally walked over him. There was a bump and the box became heavier and I realized Fred wasn't inside anymore.

"Oh, shit, where's Fred? Quick, someone, we need a light?"

"Yeah, I got it," Ted said.

"Well, light it, dammit!" I yelled frantically. Kyle was whimpering and my heart broke in sympathy, but there was no time to console him. Fred screamed from behind me, his voice muffled now that he was outside in the parking lot and I realized he had fallen to the ground after being sliced in the foot and we had inadvertently walked right over him.

"Good God, Fred!" I yelled. I dropped the box to the ground, as there weren't enough of us to hold it up anyway and I moved to the rear flap. Pushing it open on the small hinges connecting it to the wall; I could see Fred rolling around on the ground with more than a dozen scorpions on him. I could only watch in horror as pincers got to work, cutting up his limbs like he was a piece of meat on a butcher's table. The man screamed for help, but it was mercifully cut short when his head was severed from his body. The head rolled away and I swear the eyes still stared at me.

An old wive's tale says that if your head is severed from your body, there is still enough oxygen in the brain to last for a full thirty seconds. But as the only way to find out if this is true is kind of a one way experiment, there is really no way to tell if its true or false.

But when Fred's eyes blinked at me once and a tear rolled down one cheek, I became a believer. Then a darker shape scuttled by, and when it had retreated with its prize, the head was gone.

My heart sank with loss and I stood immobile. I could feel that fragile strain of civility and sanity slowly ebbing away like sand on the coast during a storm.

It was Michelle who brought me back to reality before I slipped so far into the void of madness I would never return.

"John, come on. John, snap out of it. He's gone. Think about Kyle."

I turned my head to stare at the small face of my son in the shadows inside the box. So innocent, so fragile. Everything happening around him was so far beyond his control.

Then Kyle did something that I never would have expected in a million years. He reached out one shaking hand and touched my cheek, wiping away my tears with his small thumb.

"It's okay, Daddy. We'll be okay. Can we go see Mommy now?"

I swallowed the massive lump in my throat and wiped my nose on my sleeve.

"Yeah, sport, let's go see Mommy." I turned to gaze at Ted's petrified face in the light of the Bic and my eyes opened as wide as they would go.

"Okay, Ted, it's only us left and that's fine. Because we are still here and I'll be dammed if we're gonna join the others. Are you with me?"

He nodded slowly, not really with me, but he would go along with whatever I said.

"Okay, then, let's go. The jeep should only be a few more feet ahead of us.

"Wait, John. The keys! Fred's got the keys to the jeep!" Michelle gasped.

My face dropped. "Oh Christ, you're right." My mind worked and spun as I tried to figure out what to do. I didn't know how to hotwire a car and looking at Ted, I was pretty sure he didn't either. I asked and got the answer I expected.

No, of course not.

Michelle shook her head, too, and I realized there was only one way left.

"All right, we need to back up and raise the bottom of the box so we can go over Fred's body. Come on, we need to do it now. Ted, get that saw and kill any of the things that are on Fred when we do this. You need to do this fast, too. Can you do it?"

Ted's mouth worked like a fishes and I'm sorry to say I slapped him across the face "Ted, dammit, can you do it?"

His eyes refocused and he nodded, taking the small circular saw off the wall. "Yeah, I can do it. Let's go already."

Nodding, I pushed Michelle to the front of the box, which was now the rear, and with a heave, I pushed up and began dragging the box back the way we'd come across the ground, scraping the bottom as I went. When I hit something, I knew it had to be Fred, or what was left of Fred. I flicked my own Bic lighter from my pocket and when I lowered the box to the ground, there was blood pooling below the edge of the box. It was Fred all right.

"Okay, get ready, Ted," I told him. Ted nodded, and with a yell, I lifted up with my legs and arms and dragged the box over Fred's decapitated corpse, dropping it down hard again when the body was inside with me. There were four of the scorpion creatures on Fred and I jumped out of the way and pushed Ted in front of me. The saw roared and Ted pulled the blade guard off the spinning blade and began swiping at the creatures. Blood squirted against the wooden walls, pitting it, and the sour smell of sulfur filled the area. Michelle covered Kyle's mouth with his shirt and did the same for herself.

Ted kept slashing; the last one was being difficult. It had jumped off Fred's dismembered body and was now on the ground, deftly avoiding the saw.

I decided this needed to end, so with Ted cornering it, I grabbed one of the spears from its hook and then jabbed it into the creature's head. The spear went in right between the pincers and the creature squealed in pain. I twisted hard and forced the spear in more, and when I hit ground with the end of the stick, I stopped.

It wasn't going anywhere though it still twitched, its dozen or more legs moving about. It made me cringe, a prehistoric fear of bugs I must have inherited from my descendants filling me with disgust.

Pieces of the other creatures were lying about and I kicked them aside. Both Ted and I had small holes on our sneakers and clothing from where yellow acid had sprayed us. Michelle and Kyle were safe because I had protected them with my body. I looked on at what was left of Fred, my neighbor for more than six years. Fred's torso was nothing but flesh-ribbons, organs sliding out in places. It was hard to believe only seconds ago this had been a man and my friend.

With the Bic lighter in my hand again, I leaned down and began fishing through Fred's pockets, some of the yellow, acidic blood stinging my flesh. I ignored it, knowing there was no other choice.

The front right pocket, where I keep mine also, was where I found the jeep's keys and I yanked them free like I'd found the Holy Grail.

"Got 'em, holy shit, I got 'em." I spun around to the three faces behind me. "Okay, great job, Ted, now let's get the hell out of here."

Ted didn't answer and I didn't need one from him, so I let him be.

Organizing Ted and Michelle, I had Kyle climb onto my back, his arms around my neck and his legs wrapped tightly around my waist. This way Michelle was free to lift. With only three of us, it would take that many just to drag the heavy box across the parking lot. The first hurdle was lifting the box over Fred's corpse and not let anymore of the creatures inside with us.

"Okay, on three," I said, and after counting, we lifted and pushed. The box went up and after a foot or so dropped back down. The creatures were taken by surprise and never had the chance to slide inside with us.

"Okay, that's great, now let's keep going."

We began to push up over our heads and drag the box, not wanting anymore fatalities by slicing pincers. This was hard as the ground was uneven and we constantly were jarred by indents in the parking lot asphalt. We would have to lift an inch or so and then keep moving.

It was when we hit something that we couldn't get by that made us stop again. I went to the front flap and peered out. The mop heads were dwindling, but there was still just enough light to see by. Behind us, the store was an inferno, flames licking through the roof. With no pressure in the water lines, there was no sprinkler system. Later, I found out the only reason we had water in the bathroom at all was because even with the water turned off, which it had been when the electricity went out, there was still enough pressure in the lines to give us tap water. Eventually that would have run out, though.

I looked out into the parking lot and then glanced down. There was a curb stone like the ones they put in front of parking spaces so people can't drive into the next spot. I looked to my left and there was Fred's jeep, waiting patiently for a driver.

"We're here, guys. I don't believe it, but we're here. We made it."

Shapes were moving about in the darkness and one scorpion as big as a large dog climbed onto the hood of the jeep and seemed to rear its head in a challenge. There were plenty more out there, and now that we were free of the stone walls of the hardware store, they would be much larger than the ones we had battled before. More like the ones that had taken George, and I knew if we wanted to get to that jeep, we would have to deal with them. In the flickering flames of the hardware store everything seemed to take on an unnatural quality, like how things looked at twilight, just before the sun would disappear for another day.

Fingering a propane tank and a spear, I closed the flap and gazed at each of the three faces in front of me.

"Okay, here's the tough part," I said, and began filling them in on what we would do next.

18

AND THEN THERE WERE THREE

"OKAY, SO IF you guys are both ready, let's do this and get the hell out of here," I said to Ted and Michelle. The keys to the jeep were in my hand and I was about to open the door on the front of the box and dash to the jeep's driver-side door.

When I did this, Ted was going to toss out every cordless tool we had with the power buttons pushed in, the tools set to high speed. Hopefully, the noise would distract any creatures near us long enough for me to get the door open on the jeep.

I smiled to Ted and then Michelle, taking her hand in mine and squeezing it.

"We're gonna do this," I told her. "You'll see. In a few minutes we'll be on the road and heading home."

But before I could leave, Kyle reached out from Michelle and wrapped his arms around my neck, hugging me with a fierce, panicky tightness that caused me to gasp.

"No, Daddy, don't go out there! The monsters will get you."

He said this with absolute terror, his voice trembling in fear, his eyes full of pent up emotion. Gently as I could, I pried his arms off me and tried to hand him back to Michelle, but he wouldn't go. He kept wiggling in my grasp and reaching for me again. "No, Daddy, I won't let you go! Stay with me in here where it's safe."

I pushed him away, more forceful this time, though all I wanted to do was hug him and never let go.

"I can't, champ. I need to go out there. It's the only way we're gonna get to see Mommy again."

"No, Daddy, I don't want you too. You'll just die like everyone else and then I'll be all alone!" Tears were rolling down his cheeks as he cried. His shoulders shook while he tried to talk, but he couldn't get anymore out.

"I'm sorry, Kyle, but I have no choice," I said almost coldly as I reached for the latch. I turned to Ted. "Get those tools ready, I'm going to open the door."

Ted stood still, staring at me with the Bic lighter in his hand so we could see one another. But instead of nodding that he would do as I asked, he shook his head no and suddenly, before I could stop him, he reached out and plucked the jeep keys out of my hand. I opened my mouth to protest, but he raised his free hand, halting me in my tracks.

"Forget it, John. Do you really think I can stand here and let you go out there now after just witnessing that? Christ, man, what kind of a man do you think I am?"

I opened and closed my mouth, not knowing what to say, not quite understanding what Ted was saying. Ted moved so close to me he could have kissed me if he wanted to.

"I'm going out there and you're gonna stay in here with Kyle and Michelle. But do what you said and keep those fuckers off me and we'll all be fine in a minute."

I didn't know what to say and I told him that in a few stuttering words.

"Forget, it John, just do your part and it won't matter who did what once we're all in that jeep and driving away."

"Okay," I said. "Good luck." I held out my hand for him and he took it, both of us holding on for longer than necessary. We locked eyes and I realized this was a really good man here. It was a damn shame it took me so long to figure it out.

Ted handed his Bic to Michelle, who held it in one hand, careful to keep her finger away from the hot metal of the wheel. Kyle was still crying, but he seemed somewhat relieved that I was staying inside the box.

I began grabbing power tools off the hooks hanging on the sides and setting them on the ground, while others I squeezed the buttons to turn them on. Each tool had a knob on its button that if turned on, would lock the tool in the on position. Noise began to grow as each drill, skill saw, and circular saw began to whine.

Ted halted next to Kyle and rubbed his head.

"You take care of your dad, now, Okay?"

Kyle sniffed, wiped his nose with his sleeve and nodded. Ted turned to me.

"You ready?"

"Yeah, Ted, I'm ready. Now don't run right out. Here," I said, handing him three tools, the drills spinning out of control. "Toss these to your right and I'll toss the rest to the left. Then wait two seconds and run for it."

He nodded that he understood.

Ted glanced at all of us one last time, and though the plan was to be in the jeep in less than a minute, the look he gave felt more like he was saying goodbye.

Something came to me then, a phrase I'd heard once when I was in church, the phrase from one of the old ladies that were always there. The old woman had said that the word goodbye really meant to go with God.

I said as much to Ted and he nodded curtly at me. "I don't really go in for that God stuff, you know, but I'll take all the help I can get right now," he said and then turned away from me.

Then he unlatched the door and tossed the power tools to the side as I did the same with the rest. He counted to three and then dashed for the jeep, and I closed and latched the door after him. There was actually a feeble light around the parking lot. Though not enough to read by, it was still more than enough for Ted to use to navigate the short area he needed to cover. It was like being in the middle of the woods with car headlights on you, but the beams were more than five hundred feet away. You could see by the dull glow, just not very well.

The reason for any light at all was because of the hardware store, which was now a blazing inferno. Flames reached up into the darkness overhead and shapes could be seen circling it like moths to a flame.

I watched Ted through the flap in the front of the door as he ran to the jeep.

It was working! The creatures were nowhere near the jeep or the box we were in, all of them having gone to investigate the noise of the tools that had suddenly sprung up nearby.

I saw Ted fiddling with the keys and he looked like a bull's-eye out there in the parking lot. Mentally, I was pushing him to find the right key and slide it into the door lock, but he kept missing. Fred had about twelve keys on his chain and at least six were for the jeep and other vehicles he owned, the others probably for his house. None were marked, so Ted had to keep trying until he found the right one.

The seconds ticked by and the power tools stopped whining as the scorpions ripped the tools to pieces with their pincers.

"Hurry the hell up, Ted," I said while I watched him work. It seemed like he'd been standing out there forever, but in fact only seconds had gone by.

Then Ted found the right one and he slid it into the lock like the fabled shoe sliding on Cinderella's foot. He cried out in success and turned to look my way, prepared to wave us on when a darker shadow than the surrounding darkness descended over him. Ted either saw the shadow or sensed something overhead, because he looked up into the inky depths of the sky, as if he could peer through the night.

"No Ted, focus man, get the door open, get inside!" I yelled, but it was too late.

As I watched in horror, frustrated by my impotence, the shape landed on top of Ted and claws the size of trash barrels hooked onto his shoulders, the tips digging deep into his body. Ted let go of the keys still in the door and began screaming, his hands reaching up to grab the claws. Blood seeped down his body, and as he was lifted into the air, blood droplets dripped from the soles of his Doc Martins to patter on the ground listlessly.

I banged my hands on the walls of the box helplessly while I watched Ted rise into the air, kicking and screaming the entire time. Just before he was out of sight of the light from the hardware store inferno, I saw some kind of beaked head lean over and cover Ted's head. The screaming stopped abruptly and the body went limp in the claws. Then the wings flapped and Ted floated away into the darkness.

I slammed my hands against the wall again and again and yelped out in pain. Michelle didn't move, not understanding what had happened yet, and I was too shocked to tell her. She kept asking me, her voice frantic, but all I did was sob. Finally, she set Kyle down next to me and pushed me out of the way to look for herself. There was nothing to see but a blood stain on the jeep's driver-side door window.

But then her eyes lit up when she saw the keys were still in the door.

"John, the keys, they're still in the door! We can still make it!"

Still in shock, I glanced out the flap again to see she was right. But I was in no condition to try for it. Something about watching Ted being yanked into the air like a child's toy by something out of the prehistoric age made me realize the futility of my situation. At that moment, I was only thinking of myself and the self pity I felt filled me to the brim. I shook my head back and forth, giving up.

"It's no use, Michelle, we're doomed. We're dead. If not now, then an hour from now, or a day, or a week. Sooner or later those things are gonna get us."

Michelle stared at me in anger and I saw my pitiful actions were enraging her. She picked up Kyle and then punched my shoulder. "Well, I'm not ready to die yet, and if you are, then you can go to Hell!" She shifted Kyle to her other hip and hugged him, holding him close to her, then she grabbed the only one pound propane tank that had been inside the box--the others had still been in the hardware store—and turned on the attached valve. When it was open, she used the Bic and lit it, the steady blue flame igniting immediately. Before I could stop her, she opened the box door and was running to the jeep.

"Come with us, John, we need you," she said while exiting the box, actually stepping over me.

Kyle screamed in fright while he bounced on her hip like a backpack, Michelle running into the night towards the jeep. Two creatures came at her and she used the flame of the torch to make them back away. Whatever these nightmares from hell were, they could die. They weren't invulnerable.

She kicked another away from her and Kyle with her shoe and then she was running to the jeep.

That was when I looked up, amazed at how far she'd gotten so fast. It was when I saw Kyle in her arms that I came back to my senses. Fear for Kyle made me grab a spear off the wall of the box and charge into the night after them.

Michelle faced the jeep's door and wrapped her hand around the keys. All she had to do was turn the key and she did so, quickly and efficiently. Her hand did not shake, she was like a rock.

Behind her, one of the dog-sized scorpions had spotted her and was already skittering across the pavement on its two dozen legs to reach her. I yelled a charge and lowered the spear just before those razor-sharp pincers reached her legs. The spear entered it in the side of the body and I pushed it out of the way. I didn't stop to finish it off, but instead turned and lunged for the jeep. The driver's door was open and Michelle was jumping inside, tossing Kyle into the front seat as she moved. Following, I dived into the jeep, reaching over myself to slam the door closed. Just as the door clicked shut, something hit the side of the vehicle, rocking the jeep on its shock absorbers.

That had been close. Too damn close.

We sat there in the jeep for less than ten seconds, but I realized there were no more attacks against the door. I reached out and Kyle jumped into my arms and I hugged him tightly. He shook in my hands, scared out of his mind, and I mumbled soothing words to him. Words mind you, I didn't feel were truthful, but once again I was doing my fatherly duty. When he'd quieted down a little, I gently pushed him off me and Michelle took him once more.

Looking over the sill of the window, I saw the creatures were still out there, but they didn't seem interested in us anymore. Michelle saw some on her side of the jeep and she looked at me with curious eyes.

"Why did they stop?" Then she added in a whisper. "Not that I'm complaining."

I shook my head back and forth. "Maybe they can't hear us or smell us inside here?" I said in a whisper.

I realized we had none of the food and water we'd packed inside the wooden box with us and all I had for a weapon was the gun still in my back pocket, and so far I kept forgetting it was there as I wasn't used to carrying a firearm. Not to mention that if the creatures were attracted to sound, then a gun would only make things worse by calling them to me like a dinner bell each time I fired it. But the missing food was serious. If we got stuck out on the road we were in big trouble. I turned my head to look at Michelle and Kyle, my gaze lingering on Michelle.

"That was pretty damn dangerous what you just did. What the hell were you thinking?"

Her blue eyes flashed annoyance. "I was thinking you were collapsing from shock and I wasn't about to die in there, nor let Kyle die with you."

I nodded, understanding perfectly. "Well, despite that what you did was totally insane, thank you for doing it."

She grinned then and Kyle nuzzled her neck. He was petrified, his eyes glossy. Being outside in the darkness like that had really freaked him out. Not that I blame him in the least. The poor kid, I couldn't even imagine what he must have been going through.

We sat on the driver's seat for another ten minutes, feeling relatively safe. Around us, the scorpion creatures moved about, some still feeding on what was left of Fred. Dark shapes flew by silently in the sky, and if it wasn't for the flames of the hardware store, I would never have known they were up there.

Eventually we calmed down enough to decide it was time to try and leave. I sat up in the seat and stared at the madness surrounding me.

"You guys ready?" I asked.

Michelle swallowed hard, her throat moving up and down. Kyle was in her lap, his eyes closed. I think he might still have been in shock, but I didn't know what to do about it, so I let him rest. I think he might have been sleeping and I wondered if that was a relief mechanism. Lord knows, I wished I could close my eyes and just pretend everything was fine and I was safe. Michelle was slowly rubbing Kyle's back while she said soothing words to him. I wondered if she knew they were helping me, as well.

What is it about a woman's voice, telling you that things will be all right that is so calming? Perhaps it has to do with mother issues most men have. Even if they won't admit it to themselves or anyone else.

I turned the key in the ignition and the engine turned over immediately. I backed up into the first lane and then spun the wheel. I drove the length of the parking lot, still able to just see by the fires behind me, and when it became too dark to navigate by, I turned on the jeep's headlights.

A few of the creatures were in the road and they scattered like pigeons when you frighten them as you walk through the park. I guess they didn't like the headlights. Made sense, if they lived in perpetual darkness their entire lives, however long those were, then the bright lights should cause them displeasure or maybe even pain.

Turning out of the parking lot and onto the main road, I began the journey home, and hopefully, by some divine miracle, Karen was waiting for me safe and sound.

19

BRAVE NEW WORLD

WHILE I DROVE down the lonely road with only the headlights of the jeep to illuminate the landscape around me, I thought back to a story my father told me when I was younger. My father was in the Navy. He had served two full terms before leaving the service with an honorable discharge. He'd told me he'd left because he'd met my mother and didn't want to have to leave her constantly when his boat would set sail. I say boat because my father was stationed on a submarine out of Norfolk, Virginia.

His boat, as the men called it, was a fast attack submarine, and he often told me choice tidbits of his travels around the world. In his two tours of duty, he had visited most of Europe and more than half of the United States, and he told me out of all the experiences he'd experienced, there had been only one that had always stuck with him.

He explained to me how, when a submarine is coming into port, it has to surface more than eight hours before entering the canal that will bring it home to its berth. Cruising on top of the ocean, the submarine would slice through the water like a knife.

Whenever the boat would be on the surface of the water, a man would be stationed in the sail of the vessel at the top where there was a perch. The sail, if you don't know, is that fin that rises straight up just a little back from the bow of the vessel. If you've ever seen a submarine crash through the ice in Antarctica or Alaska, that is the sail that pops up.

My father was on the midnight watch one night and he told me how in awe he'd been the first time he climbed up the ladder inside the sail. He'd come out at the top and had looked around at the dark sky and had seen nothing but blackness for as far as the eye could see. He then told me how, at that moment in time, how truly small he had felt; so insignificant compared to the vast ocean surrounding him.

He told me there was no way to truly describe what it was like to be in the middle of the ocean with nothing on all sides for miles and miles but complete, oppressive darkness. With the exception of the few stars overhead, he would have thought he had been swallowed into a black hole where no light ever existed. The only lights at all, he told me, were on the submarine itself, the running lights and one spotlight that faced down to the rear of the vessel. He'd said it was absolutely inspiring.

He then tried to explain to me that the average man, woman and child has never been able to stand outside in the night air and truly experience what it's like to be surrounded by nothing but darkness. Living in civilization, there is always some ambient light nearby, whether it's from a nearby city, streetlamps, or simple car headlights. What I mean to say is that even at the height of the night, with no moon in the sky and the stars shrouded by clouds, if you step outside, it is never truly dark.

Well, as the jeep moved through the darkness, I believed at that moment I understood the picture my father had been trying to portray to me, with the exception that I wasn't fortunate enough to have even the stars or moon to guide me.

They were all gone, vanished like a magician's trick gone horribly wrong.

Now that the hardware store was far behind us and the flames were swallowed in the darkness, there was absolutely no ambient light around us. Even the headlights of the jeep barely pushed away three feet of the never-ending night. It was like the air itself was absorbing the light. Wrecked cars were all around us and seemed to crouch in fantastic poses, like a Daliesque vision from Hell.

On all sides of us there was nothing but inky blackness. No shapes, no lights, absolutely nothing. Only my pale reflection looked back at me from the front windshield, thanks to the glowing dashboard.

Neither of us spoke, too overwhelmed with what we were witnessing. Inside the hardware store, we had walls around us, and there had always been some light to push away the gloom, whether it was by candle or cigarette lighter or the oil lanterns. But now, all alone on the road, I truly believed we were the only ones left alive in the city, hell, perhaps the world.

The jeep rolled on and soon we reached the rotary that Fred had forced his way though less than forty-eight hours ago. Wrecked cars and pieces of human beings were everywhere, blood coating windows and doors of the stranded vehicles.

There was barely any room for us to make it through the rotary, and at one point I had to give up and back up and drive around the entire area, using back roads I knew like the back of my hand.

While we drove, Michelle and I stared out our windows at the houses lining the streets. We could barely see them, the headlights casting a paltry light, but we were able to see enough, especially if I turned the front of the jeep so that the headlights were now aimed directly at a home or building.

What we saw made us cringe in fear.

Some of the houses were crushed and others had been on fire, and were now nothing but burnt-out husks. Some were still intact with the exception that all the windows were shattered and front doors stood open like someone had left and would be back in a few minutes. The scorpion creatures were everywhere, crawling in and out of the windows and doors like it was their nests. Some carried unidentifiable bloody, body parts in their pincers. Shadows of the creatures moved around the jeep, but didn't seem to be interested in us. Overhead, in the headlights beams, on the edge of where the light pierced the darkness, large shapes could be seen flying in the air. Others seemed to be resting on the top of rooftops, and I wondered if they could see me while I drove by. The ones flying overhead, thankfully, also left us alone.

One time, as I made the turn onto Broadway, we saw something huge, or better yet, heard something huge. It was as large as a school bus. Not knowing what to do, I slammed on the brakes and turned off the headlights, only leaving the parking lights on. The ground shook and I reached for Michelle and Kyle while the massive creature trundled towards us, its multiple legs churning up the asphalt and knocking vehicles aside like a tank. I felt the vibration of its movement in my teeth as it moved by us, small bits of gravel pelting the front of the jeep as it rolled by the front grille and receded down the opposite end of the street to become lost in the darkness.

It had been one of the scorpion creatures, only massive, and I finally had my answer as to how big they grew.

I sat there in the middle of the road, the engine idling for another three minutes, before I decided it was safe to move again. With the tires crunching on gravel and debris, we continued onward.

It took almost an hour to get to my house; a ride that would normally only take seven or eight minutes. The going was rough the entire time. More wrecked vehicles cluttered the roads and more than once I had to drive on people's lawns just to get by.

It was Hell on earth; or as close to Hell as I believe someone still alive and walking the earth could get to witnessing it. The city I knew so well had been transformed into a deadly wasteland where monsters from my worst nightmares existed and fed on humanity. No, wait, actually from what I've seen, these creatures of horror fed on anything they could find.

As we made the journey through the wrecked city, I never saw one cat, dog, rat, mouse, bird or any other living creature from my world, animal or human. Just that one wounded dog for only a split second. Oh, wait, I haven't said anything about the dog yet, did I.

When I said we saw no one else alive, I was only partly truthful.

Once, halfway to my home, we spotted a dog. In the darkness, I couldn't see what kind it was, but I think it was one of those Huskies or Alaskan malamutes; the kind that Eskimos use and that look like wolves and are a thousand bucks a pop at the pet store. We heard it first and I slowed the jeep down to try and hear better. I once heard if you open your mouth when you're trying to hear something faint, it works better.

The dog sounded like it was in pain and I flicked the headlights to high beam, hoping to pierce the veil of darkness in front of the jeep.

With the brighter illumination, the dog hobbled into view in front of the vehicle. It was twenty feet away, and even with the high beams,

I could barely see it.

At first, I wondered how a dog had managed to survive out here all alone. The scorpions and bat creatures appeared to be everywhere and I would have assumed the dog would have been attacked almost immediately.

I received my answer as I stared at the animal caught in my headlights. It was missing its two rear legs and was trying to drag itself towards us. Michelle raised her right hand to her mouth in shock and sadness and covered Kyle's eyes with her other hand. I could only stare in horror as the poor animal tried to drag itself towards the jeep. The closer it got, the louder its whimpering became.

The poor animal hadn't managed to crawl more than five feet towards me before a shadow transformed into one of the scorpions. This one was big, I'd say as big as a full-grown horse, and it ran at the dog, scooped it up in its pincers and then scuttled away while I stared dumbfounded. The dog squealed once and was silent.

The entire incident happened in less than five seconds, and despite the knowledge there was nothing I could have done, it was still heartbreaking. I imagined if Kyle was somehow set to wandering out there alone. How long would he make it until a dark shape solidified out of the darkness to take him screaming into the night?

Michelle and I sat staring out the window while Kyle fussed to be set free from her embrace. I nodded that she could let him go and Kyle climbed off her, his head looking out into the darkness.

"I thought I heard a doggy. Was that a doggy, Daddy?" He asked, his eyes searching the void.

"Yeah, champ, it was," I said weakly. I still had the image of the dog being scooped up and hauled away.

"Where'd the doggy go?"

I shook my head, not really knowing what to tell him. The dark around the jeep felt like it was pressing in on me. I sat there, staring at the dashboard while the engine ticked away quietly as it idled.

"Daddy? Are you all right? Are we going home now?"

I pulled myself together, though I believe it was only on the outside. Inside my mind, another crack in the dam was widening. I wondered how long I could make it until the dam of my sanity finally exploded outward and washed me away like an uprooted tree.

I looked at Kyle's cherub-like face and smiled. It was forced, but he believed it.

"Yes, Kyle we're going home right now."

I shifted the transmission into drive and we continued on, the tires rolling over debris. Thank God Fred had purchased a four wheel drive or I don't believe we would have made it all the way back to my house. I think we would have ended up trapped somewhere out in the darkness.

No one spoke after the dog incident and I felt Michelle's hand on my shoulder, trying to comfort me. I touched her hand with mine and squeezed gently, letting her know I appreciated it.

Looking back to everything that happened, I don't even know how me and Kyle would have survived without her help and courage.

Once again, I began to think about how awkward it was going to be with her and my wife together, but that would be something to deal with later. For now, I needed to concentrate on the road, which was growing worse. A large transit bus had blocked the road ahead of the jeep and my headlights cast the bus' windows in its silvery light. Every window on the bus was shattered and covered with something brown, and rags of torn clothing, also stained, hung from the corners of the window frames, lying listlessly in the night. The stains had to be dried blood, but once again there were no bodies. The scorpion creatures were there, of course, crawling around inside the bus and on the roof, and the sides that now resembled ant holes with the windows broken and shattered. They turned to look in my direction, but then turned away uninterested.

I was barely able to make it around the crushed and wrecked bus, and the jeep scraped on both sides. The bus bumper was on the left and a telephone pole on the right. The sidewalk was choked with debris from a collapsed store front, so there was no going around. With a screech of torn metal, the jeep squeezed through and we all breathed a sigh of relief.

Leaving the silent transit bus behind, we continued on, hoping nothing else would obstruct our path.

My house was only a few streets away and we would be there in no time.

20

THE END

FIFTEEN MINUTES LATER, I turned onto my street and slowed to a stop two houses down from mine. In the headlight beams of the jeep, everything looked different. What I could see appeared washed out, as if any color had faded with the disappearing sun. Most of the houses on the street were similar to the ones I had already driven by after leaving the hardware store. Gaping openings beckoned from within damaged and broken buildings.

The creatures had been here, as well. Not that I expected anything different, but I had hoped.

Kyle was sitting up now. He recognized where we were and his eyes were darting back and forth in expectation of seeing our home. Slowly, I took my foot off the brake and rolled the remaining distance. I turned the jeep so that the headlights were aimed directly at my front porch and I rolled onto my front lawn so I could get us as close as possible to the porch stairs. I ended up stopping about fifteen feet away, a few boulders that littered my yard restraining me from trying to get closer.

The first thing that gave me hope Karen might be okay was the windows of my home. They were all still intact and my front door was closed. But then I looked to the houses to the left and right of mine, and saw, they too, appeared unharmed. But when the light of the headlights struck the other homes, I saw I was very wrong. True, some of the windows were still intact, but others were not, and I saw pincers staring out at me, twitching in expectation of me leaving the jeep.

I put the jeep in park and turned off the engine, but left the electrical on so the dashboard would give us some light to see by. Next, I turned off the headlights and we all sat silently in the darkness of the jeep, staring out the windows. There were a few of the creatures around, but they were scattered and seemed not to notice us, and the ones in nearby homes were far enough away I was fairly confident we could get to my front door before they could reach us.

I looked at my house and then back to Michelle, who was more agitated now that we had finally reached the end of our journey.

"Are we going to go in and see Mommy now?" Kyle asked while he moved about on the seat between me and Michelle. He looked excited, like he would after a long trip we had taken and were now pulling into the driveway, home at last.

I swallowed hard, knowing the only way to safety was to leave the security of the jeep. Something inside of me whispered to me to stay in the jeep. It was safe here. Nothing would hurt me as long as I stayed in the jeep.

But I knew that was silly. We had to leave, it had to be done. Even if we wanted to stay, we couldn't live in the jeep forever. For one thing, we had no food or water. No, we had to go for it. After all, wasn't that what my goal had been the entire time I was trapped in the hardware store? To return to my home and Karen? But now that I was here, I had to admit, I was damn scared.

Remembering what happened to Ted flooded my memory and I felt myself beginning to shake with nerves. I knew we had to go now, because if I thought about it anymore, I would only chicken out.

"Okay," I said, trying to keep my voice from cracking. "When I say go, we open the doors and run for my front door. Once I get the door open we can get inside. Piece of cake."

Michelle didn't answer, only tried to smile. I could tell she felt as I did.

I leaned over Kyle and opened the glove box of the jeep, searching for anything useful. I was pleased to find a small flashlight, and I took it out, checking to make sure the batteries still worked. I silently thanked

Fred for being so pragmatic and organized. Rummaging around some more, I found a map, a disposable camera for if Fred had an accident and wanted to document it, and an old pack of Marlboros. I smiled at that. Fred was supposed to have quit smoking more than a year ago. Margie would kill him if she knew these were in the jeep. But then I realized it didn't matter anymore and my smile faltered as I thought about Fred's dismembered corpse in the hardware store's parking lot.

My heart was thumping in my chest and I felt like I was going to scream. A small part of me wanted to just open the door of the jeep and run screaming into the night until one of the creatures caught and killed me. At least it would be over fairly quick, providing they were able to slice a main artery or something.

I closed my eyes and let out a heavy breath, trying my best to control myself. I had to be strong, for Kyle, if for no other reason.

"Okay, are you ready, Michelle?"

She tried to chuckle, but it was completely bravado. In the gloom of the dashboard lights, I could see she was petrified.

I reached over and cupped her face with my hands, Kyle looking at me with confusion. Why was I doing this? This wasn't mommy. He had only seen me touch mommy like this.

"Hey," I said to her with a slight grin, "We'll be okay. It's only a few feet to the porch and then we're inside. You'll see. You're gonna be fine."

Tears were brimming in her eyes and she wiped them away.

"You promise?" She whispered hoarsely and in her eyes I saw the young woman I had fallen in love with all those years ago.

"Yeah, honey, I promise." I glanced down at Kyle. "You ready, champ?"

"You bet, Daddy, let's go see Mommy. I bet she's scared with all the monsters around."

I chuckled and this time it was genuine. "Yeah, sport, I bet she is." Then I got serious and I picked Kyle up and set him on my lap. "Okay, Michelle, I'll take Kyle with me. You just worry about yourself. Now, they're spread out pretty good out there and if we run to my porch, we should be inside before they know we're even out here, okay?"

She nodded; her face filling with fear. There was nothing I could do. She had to make the run for the porch on her own, I couldn't hold her hand.

"Okay," I said, turning off the electrical and dashboard lights. A creature of habit, I put the keys in my pocket. I didn't know if I would be back for the jeep again, but there was no reason to kill the battery. "Okay," I said again, "on three. One," I reached for the door handle, Kyle wrapped his arms around my neck and I held him with my right arm. My hand also held the flashlight, but I wanted to keep it off, not wanting to alert the creatures what we were doing. "Hold on tight, Kyle, we're gonna run real fast." He nodded that he understood. "Two," I said and slowly cracked the door, but didn't open it yet. Michelle had done the same on her side and I could hear her breathing coming hard and fast. The dome light came on over my head and I quickly slapped it off. "Three!" I yelled and opened the door and ran across my lawn to my front door. I looked behind me, but Michelle wasn't following. Her pants had caught on the edge of the door where some of the metal had been gouged and ripped by the telephone pole when I had squeezed by the transit bus.

She was stopped short and had to fiddle with the material until I heard it rip.

Meanwhile, I had continued to race across my lawn and was now safely on my porch. I set Kyle down and I turned on the flashlight to help her see.

She managed to pull herself free and a large piece of her pants ripped, her creamy skin peeking out. She turned and ran for me. I had the flashlight on her face, and though I should have had my keys out and sliding them into the lock, I felt I needed to see her safely across the lawn.

Her hair was flowing behind her and her arms were flailing in front of her while she ran.

"Come on, Michelle, you're almost there," I called softly, not wanting to yell.

When she was no more than six feet from my porch stairs, I saw her face soften. She knew she was going to make it.

Neither I nor she ever saw the darker shape solidify out of the deeper darkness to her left and charge directly towards her.

I heard the thunder and turned the flashlight in time to see a large scorpion the size of a cargo van come charging out of the dark. Its pincers opened wide and before Michelle could do more than look on with surprise, the creature snatched her up and was moving away from the house. Michelle managed one bone-shattering scream and then she was gone, lost in the darkness. I could hear the thunder of the creature's legs for only a second and then that, too, faded away.

"Michelle?" I said, not comprehending what just happened. It had happened so fast. Like a bolt of lightning, there was no way to prepare for it. Blink and you missed it.

And just like that Michelle was gone.

I fell to my knees in shock. One more blow to an already fragile psyche and I tried to keep from losing my breath. I had loved her, and just like that, she was gone. No goodbye, nothing.

In the darkness of the street, shapes and shadows were emerging, the creatures now sensing I was there, exposed and fragile. They were all sizes. Some were small like rats and others were the size of full-grown horses and cows.

Kyle was pulling on my arm, telling me to get up, that we needed to get inside the house where it was safe, but I heard nothing. The grief flooding me was too much. I was lost in it. I couldn't move.

Kyle ran around to stare at my face, only the flashlight to see by, and yelled into my glazed eyes.

"Daddy, the monsters are coming! Daddy, what's wrong with you?"

He grabbed my face in his hands and shook me, his spittle landing on my cheeks. "Daddy, wake up, we have to get inside with Mommy!"

Mommy. That was what did it I think. There was still Karen, and Kyle. I had to save Kyle.

With Kyle's help, I got to my feet and moved to the front door. Reaching into my pocket, I grabbed my house keys and my heart stopped when they weren't there, only the keys from the jeep were there.

"What, no, this can't be, they're not here. Jesus Christ, my keys, my goddamn house keys. They're not in my pocket!"

A memory came to me then, how when I'd been lying on the rugs in the hardware store with Michelle and I had gotten an itch on my leg. I had taken my keys out and used them to scratch with. I didn't remember putting them back in my pocket. Had I set them down above my head to use later? I must have. And then we were attacked again. Oh Christ, that itch was about to cost me and my son our lives!

I was so frozen with terror and loss I never even thought about the small handgun in my back pocket. Not that it would have done much good against the thirty or so creatures that were slowly skittering across the street and from the nearby homes.

I pulled Kyle to me and I backed up as far as I could go. My back stopped when it touched the front door of the house and I waved the flashlight out into the front yard. There were no eyes to look back at me, but there were plenty of red and puckering mouths glaring back with hooked teeth glinting in the wan light of my small flashlight.

Kyle was pushing against me, terrified. He was screaming as he watched the creatures approaching. He had witnessed enough death in the past day and a half to know what was going to happen to him and me.

"No, Daddy, the monsters are gonna get me! No Daddy, don't let them!" He screamed as he shoved his head into my stomach and his legs tried to crawl up my body.

But there was nothing I could do. No matter what I wanted to happen, there was no way I could save him.

But I could spare him suffering. With shaking hands and tear-filled eyes, I lowered my hands to his neck, wrapping my left hand around his shoulder and my right around his chin. One good pull and I would snap his neck like a dry twig.

He would be dead, but it would happen instantly. No suffering. It was the least I could do for my boy.

He was crying, his shoulders shuddering in fear as the creatures slowly moved closer. They were on the lawn now, passing the jeep. They were on the front walk. I swallowed hard. I could barely see with all the tears in my eyes. I knew what was waiting for me in those dozens of razor-sharp pincers.

But if I had to kill my only son, then I really didn't care what happened to me afterward. In fact, I welcomed the ghastly creatures.

They were on the stairs now, only seconds from reaching us. I could smell their foul stench, that sweet sulfur odor, and I knew this was it. My arms tensed on Kyle's shoulder and chin as I prepared to yank and snap his neck.

"I love you, son," I said and then I…

And then the door at my back fell away and I was falling backwards with Kyle in my arms.

Before I knew what was happening, hands were dragging us into my house and when my feet cleared the threshold, the door was slammed closed. No sooner did the door close than the sounds of dozens of bodies struck the door and frame.

I still didn't know what was happening. The house was dark, but there was light coming from the cellar. It was Kyle who filled me in on what had just happened when he yelled at the top of his lungs. "Mommy, it's you! We came to save you!?"

Kyle was in the arms of a shadow and when I looked up, the flashlight still in my hand, I aimed the beam at the face above me and my jaw fell open and I swear to God my heart stopped for one brief second in shock, relief and surprise.

"Karen? Oh my God, is that really you?"

She nodded, brushing Kyle's hair with her fingers. She was squeezing him tightly and didn't want to let go.

"Of course it's me, silly. I feared the worst, John. I can't believe you're really here."

She fell to her knees and we hugged, crushing Kyle between us. He didn't seem to mind.

"I heard Kyle's voice and I thought I was imagining it," she said.

One of the front windows broke and the sound of tinkling glass filled the house. Karen looked away from me and her eyes darted to the front room.

"Shit, now they know I'm in here, and you guys, too!" She pulled me up and then pointed to the cellar door a few feet away. "Come on, John, we all need to get down into the cellar. If they don't hear us after a while, they might go away."

More windows were breaking and then the front door buckled. It was made of metal, but the frame was of wood. One or more of the large scorpions was trying to gain entry.

I was still in complete shock, but Karen took my hand, and with Kyle in the lead, we all headed downstairs into the basement. Karen was the last one to go down the stairs and she pulled the heavy, wooden door shut that divides the cellar from the first floor of the house.

In the small light of a single candle, I could see canned goods, boxes of food and bottles of water. Karen filled me in on how she knew there was something terribly wrong when the power went out and the darkness descended. She took all the food from the kitchen and brought it into the cellar. Then she hid, staying perfectly quiet.

She could hear the sounds of screaming and anguish coming from out on the street, but she stayed put. She didn't know at the time, but it was the smartest thing she could have done. When other people were going outside to see why it was pitch black out, they had promptly been attacked by the creatures, while my wife had stayed silent and hidden in our home.

When I finally came to my senses, I hugged her so hard she had to slap my back to stop me. I kissed her and she cried and her tears tasted like honey. I apologized for leaving and she told me it was all right. I had brought her son back to her and that was all that mattered. I could only imagine what she had thought while huddling in the darkness, wondering if Kyle and me were alive or dead.

After another moment, we hugged again, Kyle giggling in happiness; his family was together once again.

Whatever would happen next, we would face it together.

* * *

Above our heads, on the first floor, the creatures are now moving about. Their legs scratch the floor and they knock things from the counters as they search for the prey they saw enter days ago. I can only hope in time they will give up and move on.

More than a week and a half has past since I returned home, and they're still up there, searching. I'm beginning to think they will never leave.

Not as long as the dark reigns supreme over the earth.

While I hold my shivering wife in one arm and my sleeping son in the other, I finish writing this story in my little notebook The flashlight perched on my shoulder is slowly dimming as it prepares to go out. The batteries are almost drained and there are no new ones to replace them. The candles, too, are exhausted, Karen only managing to find a few.

As we sit in the fading light of the flickering bulb, I can feel my wife and child's fear meld with my own. There's a new sound now, as well, added to the old ones. I've been hearing the small scrapings of what resembles a thousand claws on metal and wood as the creatures try to get through the small basement windows. Add that to the hundreds more moving about overhead on the first floor and there are far too many to ever overcome if they manage to gain entry to our sanctuary.

Lying in my lap is the gun taken from the gangbanger, Slim, and I know there are only three more rounds left in it, and I wonder if there'll be enough time to use it as a last resort if the basement windows don't hold.

Tears begin to fill my eyes yet again and my vision becomes blurry. I decide I've written enough for the night--it's always night now--so I'm going to close the notebook and slide it back into my pocket to join its twin.

But I'll write a few more lines before I do this.

This is the end of my story, I'm afraid; I really don't think there's more to tell.

I found my wife safe and now we're all together again. So far we're secure in the cellar, the windows are double-paned and I don't think those things are smart enough to get in, despite their never-ending ministrations. I even made sure to spray Raid around the sills, just another way, I hope, to deter them.

I don't know what will happen next, and I guess that has to be the scariest thing of all. Fred's jeep is still on my front lawn. It has more than half a tank of gas and I suppose we could all pile into it and drive away. But the fact is; where would we go? For all I know, the entire world is nothing but darkness, or then again, maybe it's just the east coast that's affected.

I've decided there's nothing else to do and nowhere else to go. All we can do is wait and see what happens next.

The sun could come back tomorrow, bathing the world in its brilliance once more, or it may never return, leaving the world forever swallowed in eternal darkness. Either way, at least I have my family with me.

We have enough food and water with us for another three or four weeks; more if we ration it.

I'm sorry if this isn't the ending you may have hoped for, to tell you the truth, I'm not very happy with it myself, but this isn't a movie or a fantasy novel that ends with the heroes riding off into the sunset. This is the real world, and in the real world, things don't always go the way you want them to.

Besides, there's no sunset to ride into anymore, and may never be again.

When we're young, our parents tell us not to fear the dark. That what we imagine to be hidden in the shadows is only a figment of our imagination.

Perhaps at one time that was true. But times change.

In this new world of perpetual night, I'm sorry to say there is something waiting in the darkness.

Pray to God it doesn't find you.

DARK PLACES
By Anthony Giangregorio

A cave-in inside the Boston subway unleashes something that should have stayed buried forever.

Three boys sneak out to a haunted junkyard after dark and find more than they gambled on.

In a world where everyone over twelve has died from a mysterious illness, one young boy tries to carry on.

A mysterious man in black tries his hand at a game of chance at a local carnival, to interesting results.

God, Allah, and Buddha play a friendly game of poker with the fate of the Earth resting in the balance.

Ever have one of those days where everything that can go wrong, does? Well, so did Byron, and no one should have a day like this!

Thad had an imaginary friend named Charlie when he was a child. Charlie would make him do bad things. Now Thad is all grown up and guess who's coming for a visit?

These and other short stories, all filled with frozen moments of dread and wonder, will keep you captivated long into the night.

Just be sure to watch out when you turn off the light!

THE MONSTER UNDER THE BED
By Anthony Giangregorio

Rupert was just one of many monsters that inhabit the human world, scaring children before bed. Only Rupert wanted to play with the children he was forced to scare.

When Rupert meets Timmy, an instant friendship is born. Running away from his abusive step-father, Timmy leaves home, embarking on a journey that leads him to New York City.

On his way, Timmy will realize that the true monsters are other adults who are just waiting to take advantage of a small boy, all alone in the big city.

Can Rupert save him?

Or will Timmy just become another statistic.

DEAD TALES: SHORT STORIES TO DIE FOR
By Anthony Giangregorio

In a world much like our own, terrorists unleash a deadly disease that turns people into flesh-eating ghouls.

A camping trip goes horribly wrong when forces of evil seek to dominate mankind.

After losing his life, a man returns reincarnated again and again; his soul inhabiting the bodies of animals.

In the Colorado Mountains, a woman runs for her life, stalked by a sadistic killer.

In a world where the Patriot Act has come to fruition, a man struggles to survive, despite eroding liberties.

Not able to accept his wife's death, a widower will cross into the dream realm to find her again, despite the dark forces that hold her in thrall.

These and other short stories will captivate and thrill you.

These are short stories to die for.

SOULEATER
By Anthony Giangregorio

Twenty years ago, Jason Lawson witnessed the brutal death of his father by something only seen in nightmares, something so horrible he'd blocked it from his mind.

Now twenty years later the creature is back, this time for his son.

Jason won't let that happen.

He'll travel to the demon's world, struggling every second to rescue his son from its clutches.

But what he doesn't know is that the portal will only be open for a finite time and if he doesn't return with his son before it closes, then he'll be trapped in the demon's dimension forever.

ROAD KILL: A ZOMBIE TALE
By Anthony Giangregorio

ORDER UP!

In the summer of 2008, a rogue comet entered earth's orbit for 72 hours. During this time, a strange amber glow suffused the sky.

But something else happened; something in the comet's tale had an adverse affect on dead tissue and the result was the reanimation of every dead animal carcass on the planet.

A handful of survivors hole up in a diner in the backwoods of New Hampshire while the undead creatures of the night hunt for human prey.

There's a new blue plate special at DJ's Diner and Truck Stop, and it's you!

DEAD RECKONING: DAWNING OF THE DEAD
By Anthony Giangregorio

THE DEAD HAVE RISEN!

In the dead city of Pittsburgh, two small enclaves struggle to survive, eking out an existence of hand to mouth.

But instead of working together, both groups battle for the last remaining fuel and supplies of a city filled with the living dead.

Six months after the initial outbreak, a lone helicopter arrives bearing two more survivors and a newborn baby. One enclave welcomes them, while the other schemes to steal their helicopter and escape the decaying city.

With no police, fire, or social services existing, the two will battle for dominance in the steel city of the walking dead.

But when the dust settles, the question is: will the remaining humans be the winners, or the losers?

When the dead walk, the line between Heaven and Hell is so twisted and bent there is no line at all.

RISE OF THE DEAD
By Anthony Giangregorio

DEATH IS ONLY THE BEGINNING

In less than forty-eight hours, more than half the globe was infected.
In another forty-eight, the rest would be enveloped.
The reason?
A science experiment gone horribly wrong which enabled the dead to walk, their flesh rotting on their bones even as they seek human prey.
Jeremy was an ordinary nineteen year old slacker. He partied too much and had done poorly in high school. After a night of drinking and drugs, he awoke to find the world a very different place from the one he'd left the night before.

The dead were walking and feeding on the living, and as Jeremy stepped out into a world gone mad, the dead spotting him alone and unarmed in the middle of the street, he had to wonder if he would live long enough to see his twentieth birthday.

LIVING DEAD PRESS

Where the Dead Walk

www.livingdeadpress.com

DEADFREEZE

By Anthony Giangregorio

THIS IS WHAT HELL WOULD BE LIKE IF IT FROZE OVER.

When an experimental serum for hypothermia goes horribly wrong, a small research station in the middle of Antarctica becomes overrun with an army of the frozen dead.

Now a small group of survivors must battle the arctic weather and a horde of frozen zombies as they make their way across the frozen plains of Antarctica to a neighboring research station.

What they don't realize is that they are being hunted by an entity whose sole reason for existing is vengeance; and it will find them wherever they run.

DEADFALL

By Anthony Giangregorio

It's Halloween in the small suburban town of Wakefield, Mass. While parents take their children trick or treating and others throw costume parties, a swarm of meteorites enter the earth's atmosphere and crash to earth.
Inside are small parasitic worms, no larger than maggots.
The worms quickly infect the corpses at a local cemetery and so begins the rise of the undead.
The walking dead soon get the upper hand, with no one believing the truth.
That the dead now walk.
Will a small group of survivors live through the zombie apocalypse?

Or will they, too, succumb to the Deadfall.